MW01535379

The Adventures of the Wee Cave People

By
Eileen M. Foti

Bookman LLC
Publishing & Marketing

Providing Quality, Professional Author Services

www.bookmanmarketing.com

ISBN: 1-59453-489-6

TABLE OF CONTENTS

DEDICATION

This book is dedicated to -
    Chip for his love of books, Eileen for her love of small and gentle things, Danny for his love of animals and Charlie for his wonderful support and love.

THE ADVENTURES OF
THE WEE CAVE PEOPLE

CHAPTER I

By the side of the hill, and a little to the left, an opening peeks out. It appears to be a cave and the entrance is almost entirely covered with vines. The day is warm and the green tree covered hill is quiet under the afternoon sun. Coming along the path, leading to this cave, strolls a little man. He is barely six inches tall, as tall as a blade of grass standing tall on a summer's day. His name is Zip and he is dressed in a short yellow jacket making him appear to be a dandelion waving in the soft breeze. He nears the cave opening, then stops and looks around as if checking to make sure no one else is there.

As he enters the dark cave, Zip cannot see, his eyes remain accustomed to the sunlight. "Hello Zip," calls a voice from inside the cave. "Is that you Sam? It will take a few minutes to see you well."

Zip rubbed his eyes and turned toward the voice. "How are things going?"

"Very well nothing out of the ordinary has happened lately."

"Good. My eyes are clear now. I see you are enjoying your lunch. Be mindful of the enemy and do not doze off."

"That I won't."

"See you later," Zip called back as he hurried along a passageway leading from the cave entrance to a dark tunnel.

What appeared to be a simple little cave was anything but. Entering through a large doorway yards from the entrance to the cave, one enters into a world of darkness lit by candlelight. This light threw long shadows over the tunnels and walkways to bathe them in an eerie glow. Rooms branched off these tunnels as the tunnels led down into the cool earth. Zip stepped into one of these rooms for a moment to slip into a sweater. This little room holds a large selection of sweaters and shawls a person can slip into as he goes farther down the tunnel. Now that the sweater has warded off the chill, Zip was off once again.

In the distance, a small musical instrument known as an ocarina could be heard giving off its whistle-like tones, and an oboe, then a drum started beating out oodles of deep tones that made the tunnel walkway vibrate and shake.

A long spiral chute lined the walkway on one side and Zip decided to ride it down. He shot down the chute until he reached the bottom. Zip landed on his face on a large overstuffed pillow that lay at the chute's end.

He bounced a little and lost his hat before coming to a full stop.

Retrieving his hat, Zip slapped it on his head and climbed out of the pillow. As he started to walk away from the pillow, he stepped on his dangling shoe buckle and tumbled to the ground.

"You're always in a hurry, no wonder your father named you Zip," called a tiny old man with a white beard and gray bushy eyebrows.

Zip turned and smiled at the old man. "You are right, Bill. I am always in a hurry. How are you? Are you feeling well today?"

"Fine, today. It's good to see you back."

"It is good to be back."

After bidding his friend goodbye, Zip raced off again. Near the end of the tunnel, he dashed through a doorway and was showered by a ray of light. The light serves as a guide into a large room where many small people live. They silently go about their business. There is Zith, a little chubby, bearded fellow, who likes to eat and sing, but lately is not doing either of these things. Sitting next to Zith is Ben. Ben sits on a tree stump with his little bowed legs wrapped around the stump. He is usually a good-natured fellow with a ready grin, but not lately. As Zip walks over to the men they stop talking and he relates to them his walk outside of the cave. Zip enjoys going out to look around to see the rest of the world, but the others are afraid to venture outdoors.

A little lady named Gail, is busy at a low, round table making sandwiches for some children who were sitting on small, brown mushrooms. They are holding their tiny plates on their laps and staring at their elders with worried looks on their faces. The smallest child, Danny, broke the silence of the group, "Why can't we laugh and be happy again? Why can't we eat good things and dance and sing? Why are we always sad?"

Everyone stopped what they were doing and turned toward Danny.

Zip walked over to the child, followed by Zith, Ben; his wife, Sally; her father, Jack; and her brother, Joe. Zip lifted the frightened child to his knee while he made himself comfortable on a little brown mushroom. The others gathered around him.

"You are very young, Danny, and you probably do not understand what is going on, but I will try to tell you why we are troubled."

Danny swallowed hard and opened his eyes wide.

"Once we were very happy," continued Zip, "We lived in our own little world right here at the end of the cave. For hundreds of years, we lived in peace and happiness without a care in the world. We had good food - delicious salads, all kinds of mushrooms, roasted peanuts, mashed potatoes and leg of grasshopper. Oh, what great meals we had! Everyone in our world would line up at the long wooden table in the main dining room to have a feast. Each person had a chair, with his or her name carved on it, and a set of wooden knives, forks, spoons, plates, bowls and cups placed on the table before him. Those were the days."

"Tell him about the music, Zip," called Joe, "And the dancing and the singing."

"Yes, Joe, I will tell him of those wonderful times, for they were worth knowing about. Danny, you must have heard the ocarina, drum and oboe being played; well, we also had a violin - a very beautiful violin with flowers carved on the handle, and the music it made can't be described. This violin had magical powers. It would expand or contract to fit the hands of anyone who wished to play it. Belle played the violin, and no one could play it better."

"What happened to the violin?" whispered Danny, "I have not seen it."

"You have not, because it is no longer with us. Now I will tell you what happened to it. When you were a baby, we were happy and lived well, and our music was the best anywhere. Well, one night as the rain fell over the countryside, an intruder stumbled into our cave entrance. We did not have a guard there then. We did not mind the rain because we were not getting wet, but our visitor was wet, cold and grumpy. As he sat shivering in the cave he heard our music and singing coming up from the tunnel. The man was a giant with a thick black beard who stood seven feet tall. He wore clothes made of leather and boots of leather too. We think he inched his way down our tunnel, then he crept into our dining room."

Danny's eyes grew large and sparkly as diamonds.

"All at once, we noticed this stranger standing there hunched over in our dining room. Our leader, Peter, arose from his chair and walked over to meet this man. Peter offered the man some refreshments. The man said, 'Yes.' Peter gave him some food and drink. The man gulped it all down, then wiped his mouth with his coat sleeve. The stranger asked if he could hear some more of the fine music he had listened to from the top of the cave. The leader's daughter, Belle, plays the violin, Tom plays the ocarina, Chris plays the drum and Casey plays the oboe. On the signal from Peter, the quartet started to play. Music filled the room much to the delight of everyone. When the music stopped, the stranger stepped forward and grabbed the violin from Belle. The room was so quiet you could hear a mushroom drop.

Then the stranger spoke, 'My wife is having a birthday party soon and I didn't know what to buy her, but this wonderful violin will do nicely, or my name isn't Dom D. Dominic.'

Peter rushed forward again and pleaded, "Please, Mr. Dom D. Dominic, do not take our violin. It is the only one like it in the world. We have passed it along from generation to generation, and no harm has ever come to it. Our violin supplies the music for our folk dances and without it, our dancing would not be the same. If you take this violin, you will rob us of our spirit."

Dominic sneered, "It will not be harmed. My wife will love this violin and it will be a great addition to her violin collection. I will never tell her where I found this violin. She'll never know I took it from you. I will leave now, but do not follow me, or I will turn around and step on you and crush you like a dry, brown leaf."

"With that he turned and hurried up the tunnel carrying our beautiful violin," Zip paused and looked at Danny. "From that day on, we have not seen nor heard of our beautiful violin. Peter blames himself for being nice to Dominic and Belle blames herself for not holding on tighter to the violin, and everyone feels awful because none of us did anything to help.

Everything happened so quickly that no one knew what to do. So from then on, Peter has stayed in his room, and his wife, Pat, brings him his meals there. Belle stays in her room and does not come out, and she is so fair and lovely. Peter was too afraid to have a search party go after Dom D. Dominic for fear that someone would be injured."

Zip swallowed hard. Then he continued, "So you see, Danny, everyone is still upset and depressed about the loss of our violin. We do not sing or eat any big feasts or dance any more. Things are not the same without our wonderful violin." Zip bowed his head.

Danny looked from face to face. He noticed many of the women cried. Most of the men hung their heads and looked sad.

"Why not go and reclaim our violin?" asked Danny.

"We have thought about searching for our violin, but that is not going to be easy," sighed Zip, "Dominic is so much larger than we are."

"But, my father has often said something worthwhile is never done easily," said Danny, gesturing with his hands. "Living this way is not easy either."

Zip looked at the child, "You are right, but what can we do? We are much smaller than Dom D. Dominic, his wife and friends. How could we fight them? How could we hope to win?"

"We are on the side that is good and honest. If we try, we can win back our violin and live well again. I'm not too sure I remember the feasting on leg of grasshopper, but I would like to try it. I'm sure the rest of the kids here feel as I do."

Zip glanced around. Slowly he hoisted Danny and placed him on the floor. "What is the decision, men? Should we finally search out Dominic and retrieve our violin, or shall we live in gloom the rest of our lives and our childrens' lives?"

One by one, the men turned and mumbled to each other. Finally, they asked, "Who will go after our violin? How many men will it take?"

Zip answered, "I will take on the responsibility of tracking down our violin, but of course, I will need about five good men."

"Then we accept the challenge and will get back what is rightfully ours." said the men as they waved their arms in the air."

Zip walked into Peter's room. In a little while, Peter came out holding onto Zip's arm.

"Three cheers for Peter!" cried Zith.

"Hip, hip, hooray!" cried the group.

"I should not receive cheers; it is Zip who should receive them," smiled Peter.

All at once voices cheered for Zip.

Belle, along with her mother came out of her room. Zip hurried to her side. She said, "I have heard of your plan, and I would be most happy to play our violin again."

"For you, Belle I would try anything." Belle's eyes sparkled.

Zip picked out five good men, Zith, Ben, Joe, Tom and Chris. Each one slowly stepped forward. Their faces showed no expression. Then they grinned their approval.

Zip packed a map to help them find their way and after deciding what food and tools to take with them, they all tied a length of rope onto their belts and retired for the night, for tomorrow would be the beginning of their exciting and possibly dangerous adventure. Finally, with the return of their violin their spirit would be renewed and they all would be happy again.

FAREWELLS

CHAPTER 2

The next morning, very early, Zip, Zith, Ben, Joe, Tom, Chris, Peter and Belle gathered around the breakfast table. The men's dishes nearly overflowed with cereal, made from mashed mushrooms and milk. Belle gave them extra so they would have plenty of energy for their trip.

"Do you have any idea where Dom D. Dominic can be? Where does he live? Is it far from here? Don't forget, Dominic has long legs and can take bigger steps than we can. The distance he traveled may be too long for us to cover with our short legs," frowned Peter.

"Well, if he came here to our cave then he could not live too far away. We will find him, even if it takes longer for us to find his home. Then we will take back our violin," shouted Zip, as he gleefully jumped into the air.

"Yeah," chorused the others.

"Do not be hasty. Make sure of your position before approaching Dominic. He is seven feet tall, his arms are full of muscles, his hairy chest is extremely wide like a tree, and he is very clever," expressed Peter.

"We will be careful," confirmed Ben, with his jaw tightly set.

"He won't fight with us because we will be as quiet as possible when we retrieve our violin," Chris announced confidently.

"I can't wait to see our violin again," admitted, Tom.

"Finish your breakfast before it is cold," coached Belle, "You need something warm in your middles."

Zip smiled at Belle and felt sad to be leaving her, but if they were to get the violin back they had to vacate the cave, get on with this hazardous journey, then return safely home.

After eating, the men left the table to pack their tools, food, clothes, rope and candles they were taking with them. Each man placed a small knap-sack on his back, a hat upon his head and heavy boots on his feet. The men lined up for inspection. Peter walked along in front of the men and looked each man in his eyes as he shook his hand.

When he came to Zip, he said, "This is a brave thing you and the men will do. Our whole community feels very proud of you. Even if you do not return with our violin, we will be grateful to you for trying."

"Thank you," Zip said, readjusting his knap-sack as he spoke.

The little party made its way to the cave entrance. Belle called to Zip, who sauntered over to her.

"I know you will bring back the violin. The first song I play will be for you," blushed Belle.

"I have always loved you, Belle. I hope some day to make you my wife," nervously said Zip.

"Upon your return, I will give you my answer," whispered Belle. She kissed Zip on the cheek, then ran back into the tunnel.

"All right, men, let us be on our way," bellowed Zip, and off they marched.

Peter remained at the entrance of the cave for a long time after their departure, as he pondered the years wasted by not attempting this rescue sooner. He was sure the right men went on this mission and knew they were doing the right thing and hoped for Zip's safe return.

Thus began the quest for the violin!

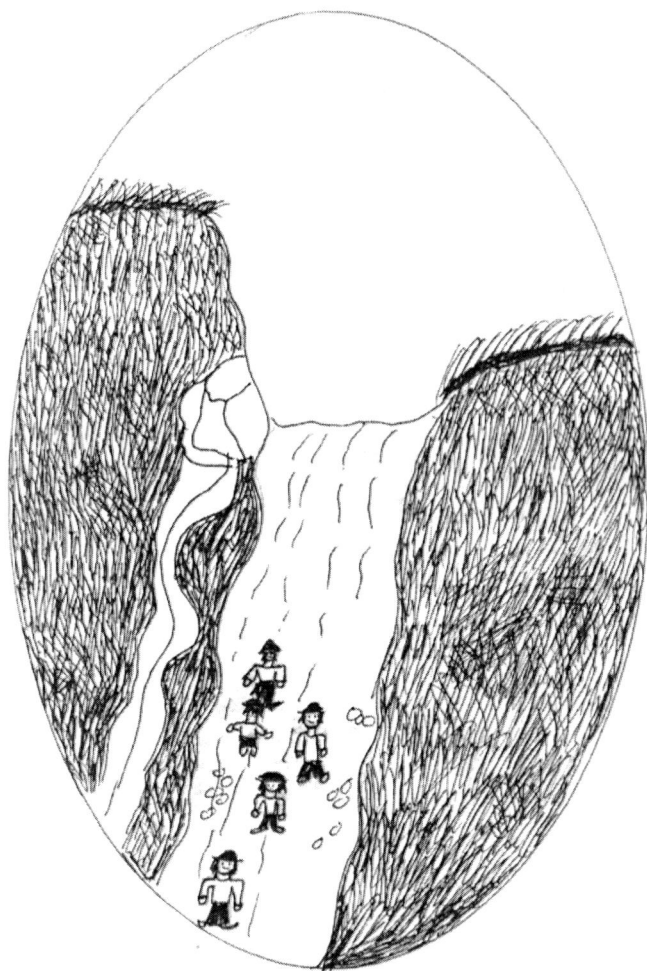

THE JOURNEY BEGINS

CHAPTER 3

As Zip led the way down the path, Ben asked, "In which direction shall we go? We don't know exactly where Dom D. Dominic lives."

"At the end of this path, we will choose our new direction. We must be careful not to make a wrong turn, or we may never see our violin again," Zip retorted, "Or our cave, either, for that matter."

They walked down the hill. Ben kicked at the round pebbles as he walked. Zith hummed a tune, while the others silently inspected the path.

"At least the weather is good today, nice and sunny," said Zip, as his eyes looked up to the sky. "It would have been a bad day to start our trip if it had been raining."

As men who could scarcely look a chipmunk in the eye, Zip being the tallest at six inches, the path seemed endless. Their little legs grew tired, as the knap-sacks became heavier.

Zip noticed the men's mounting discomfort. "Let's not complain; instead, let's keep walking, for the sooner we retrieve the violin, the sooner we can get home again."

Finally around three in the afternoon the men reached the bottom of the hill. They slithered their sacks down their backs and looked up at the hill. It seemed so far from where they now stood to the cave entrance.

"Crackers, that was some walk!" Joe sank to the ground. "My legs are feeling like two concrete drums. I think we should sit for awhile."

"Good idea," answered Zip, "Let us sit and decide just where we will go from here."

Tom built a fire and said, "I will act as cook on this trip if that is all right. I like to cook. Let me make some lunch."

Tom picked some greens from the side of the path and placed them in a pot with a little water from his canteen. He then added mushrooms and spices, stirred the mixture well and covered the pot. Next, he took some wafers from his sack and spread jelly on them. When the lunch was ready, the men took their plates from their sacks and stood in line by the fire. Tom proudly ladled each man a generous portion of mushroom stew, and gave each a wafer with jelly because he knew these men loved sweets. He then poured the rest of the stew into his plate.

When they had eaten, Zip exclaimed, "I think there is no doubt Tom should be our cook. He really has a way with fresh greens and mushrooms. They were seasoned and cooked just right."

"Thank you," Tom said, as he lowered his head.

The others clapped their approval.

Zip took a pencil and the map out of his sack. "Let us chart our way. This is an old map Peter gave to me. It has been passed down for generations. We must use this to guide us and hope the land has not changed since the map was made. We really do not know what lies ahead for us. We could run into monsters, one kind or another."

As Tom washed the dishes and the cooking pot, the other men crowded around Zip. The map was placed on the grass for all to see.

"This is where we are now, Zip pointed at a spot on the map. "We just came down this path from the hill. Now which way to go? If we walk to the left, there is a forest with great, tall trees. If we walk to the right, there is a lake, deep in the middle and shallow around the sides. Living under the ground as we do, we are not good swimmers; therefore, I think we should head through the forest. We don't know what we may find there, but I think it is our best bet. Does everyone agree?"

"What is at the other side of the forest?" asked Chris.

"No one from our community has ever gone there, so I don't know. As you can see the map ends after the forest," replied Zip.

"It is true we don't swim well," reinfoced Zith.

"I'm all for the forest," cried Joe. "Then we can see just what comes after it and add it to our map. It will be a long walk to the end of the forest. According to our map, an inch equals a mile in distance."

Tom sidled up behind the others and observed, "What if a witch or goblin lives there? We may be finished."

"Well," said Zip, "If we must fight a witch or goblin, so be it, but we must try to get our violin back.

Let us vote upon it. All in favor of the forest route, raise your hands."

Four hands went up. Then, slowly, Tom too raised his hand. One hand was missing.

"Well, I don't know if I like the forest route. I never fought a witch and I have never even seen a goblin!" Joe stated as he shifted his weight from one foot to the other.

"Do you have a better plan?" asked Zip.

"No," shrugged Joe.

"Then join us and hope for the best," chorused the men.

"What if our route is the wrong one?" asked Joe.

"What if it isn't," bellowed Zith.

"All right, I'll join you, but I hope we are right," sighed Joe.

"Good, then the voting is over. We will spend the night here, as it is getting dark, then in the morning, we will start for the forest," declared Zip.

Taking the pencil, Zip traced a line from the path to the forest. Then, he folded the map and put it in his jacket pocket.

The men slept around the fire and dreamed of witches, goblins and trees.

THE MEN MEET MR. BLUEJAY

CHAPTER 4

The break of day found Tom preparing a yummy, warm breakfast for the men. The aroma of fresh brewed coffee awakened them. After a few stretches and yawns, the men sat down to eat. The coffee tasted superb, as did the pancakes, smothered in honey, while the mushroom cereal were excellent. These men love to eat and enjoy every morsel.

After finishing every bite of their nourishing breakfast, the men packed up their bedrolls and dishes and made ready to leave. Zip, holding his map, stepped forward and said, "If anyone wishes to return to the hill, he is free to do it now before we move into the forest."

Glances shifted from one face to another face, but no one spoke.

"Then we are still all together through thick or thin, through failure or success?" rallied Zip.

"We are," screamed the men.

"Let us start then. We will come to the forest soon, so be alert, as we don't know what we will find there," warned Zip.

The day is fair and the blue sky played host to some white fluffy clouds.

After walking for an hour, the men saw the forest straight ahead of them. The trees were the tallest they had ever seen.

"What if Dominic is hiding behind the trees? He would surely crush us if he stepped on us," whispered Joe.

Zip cautioned, "Stay together now. We don't want to lose anyone in the forest. Don't worry, Joe, I don't think Dominic is just waiting for us in the forest."

"Crackers!" shrieked Joe, "I never knew trees could grow so high!"

Cautiously, they walked to the mouth of the forest and stopped.

"We will go in this direction," pointed Zip, "Be careful of tree roots. Some of them are sticking up out of the ground. If you can't crawl under them, go around them, but be careful not to fall and get hurt."

As the men trudged into the forest, the day became darker. When they looked up at the sky, they saw the foliage of the trees prevented the sun from shining through.

"I see many birds flying around up there," declared Tom, "Do you think they will bother us? Do you think they like to eat wee people like us?"

"I am sure they will not bother us, Tom," reassured Zip, "Their songs are cheerful and beautiful."

Just then, a bluejay swooped by and dropped a big, red flower on Tom. Tom fell to the ground and covered his eyes. The other men laughed because Tom looked so funny lying there under a large flower.

Tom opened his eyes and saw the flower and smelled its rich fragrance. He felt foolish, but relieved. The flower fell away from Tom as he struggled to get back on his feet. The bluejay came to rest on a tree branch just above Tom and cawed down at him.

Tom said, "Thanks for the flower; it's a thing of beauty. I know you meant no harm, but you almost scared me to death."

The bluejay cocked his head from side to side while listening to Tom speak, then he flew away. Again, the men laughed, but this time, Tom laughed with them.

They came upon a bubbling stream tumbling over jagged brown rocks. The men put their knap-sacks down, and took out their tin cups, and dipped them into the water for a drink. It tasted sweet and cold.

"Why don't we soak our feet a spell?" asked chubby Zith, "This walking is making my feet hurt."

"If we stop too many times, we will never get our violin back. Let's skip this waterfall and walk on to the next one," replied Zip.

"All right. It was only a suggestion," shrugged Zith.

"How many miles does this forest cover?" questioned Ben.

"At least twenty miles," explained Zip.

"Let us all sing while we walk along," suggested Zith, "It helps the time go by."

"We are mountainmen
And live underneath the ground,
We were born and raised there,
But never moved around.

Now we are out hunting
To take back our violin,
We will gladly bring it back
And sport a big, big grin."

The men sang in a chorus as they tramped along.

"How long have we been walking?" asked Chris, "I do not think we can reach the end of the forest all in one day."

"Of course we can't," uttered Zip, "It will take us a long time before we reach the last tree of this forest. We are making good time, and pretty soon, we will rest."

"Oops," cried Tom, as he fell over a rock and landed in a puddle. When he lifted his head out of the puddle, a little rider perched upon it. It was a frog that was swimming around, before Tom got there. The tiniest frog the men ever seen now looked very excited as he rode upon Tom's head. Tom felt something move and hesitantly reached up to feel what was there. When Tom touched the frog, the startled creature jumped off Tom's head and buried itself in the puddle again.

The men roared with laughter, and Zip decided to stop for lunch so Tom could calm down. Tom slouched to the ground, as if falling apart at the seams.

After a short time, Tom cooked up another pot of greens that was just as delicious as the last pot.

"Tell me, do you like to stick your head into puddles Tom?" mimicked Joe, as he bent down to the ground.

"Do you have a pet frog?" Chris grinned.

Tom gave them an embarrassed look and covered his face with his hands.

Ben put his arm around Tom "I think Tom is a good sport. He has taken enough kidding from us."

"Three cheers for Tom," cried Zith.

The smiling men cheered. The men huddled around Tom and told stories, shared jokes, and all had a good time.

As the sun blocked the trees, the forest floor grew very dark, even though it was not yet late.

"Hurry and pack, men, so we can cover a little more distance before bedtime," called Zip.

Once again, the men packed, struggled into their knap-sacks and started walking along the forest floor.

"Let every man have his candle ready in case we need more light; we don't want to trip over roots," called Zip, as he nervously watched ahead.

The men always enjoyed the aroma as the scented candles burned, some smelled like pine trees, some like strawberries, and some like lavender.

"Do not light them until we need them," Zith warned, "We don't want to waste them."

So on they went, singing, humming and kicking pebbles, but advancing with each step.

Joe picked up some acorns and found that he could spin them like tops, so he placed them in his knapsack for all the children in his mountain home. Only the acorns that fell from the trees with a little piece of the stem still on the top could be used to spin.

If the stem was missing the acorn would wobble and not spin.

The men lit their candles as night fell around them. Darkness slowly crept over them and the candles glowed brightly, throwing shadows across their paths.

Finally, Zip said, "This looks like a good place to spend the night; look Zith, another waterfall. Now you may soak your feet."

Zith really moved quickly to take off his knapsack and run over to the waterfall, pulled off his shoes and stick his feet into the cool swiftly moving water. This was not easy for Zith to do because he is chubby.

"Ah! This feels terrific," sighed Zith, "Why not join me, Tom?"

Tom waved his hand and said, "I had enough water for one day."

This answer prompted much laughter.

"Are there any fish in that water?" Ben cautiously asked, "Watch they don't bite your toes off!"

As Zith yanked his feet up out of the water, he lost his balance and fell in with a splash.

"Help, help! I can't swim!" cried Zith, floundering in the water.

The men stood spellbound. Then Zip sprang into action, "Quickly grab that tree branch and push it out to Zith. He can hold on to it until we pull him ashore."

The force of the water flowing from the waterfall was so strong, the men had a terrible time tugging, and pulling before they finally succeeded in pulling Zith ashore.

"Come, come now, let's settle down for the night," said Zip exhaustedly, "Or come morning we will be too tired to move on. Zith, relax and get some rest."

The men washed in shivering silence, for the running water was icy cold touching their bodies.

After washing up, Tom built a fire and the men crowded around it for warmth. The men spoke about their cave and relatives and after a few tales, the men, one by one, nodded off to sleep.

LEAVING ZITH BEHIND

CHAPTER 5

In the morning, the men awoke to the cawing of their friend, Mr. Bluejay. He made a few low passes over them to make sure they were awake, then perched on a tree branch to watch the men.

"Is that your 'feathered delivery bird' back again, Tom? Did he bring you another bloom?" teased Ben, with a smile on his face.

"I-I-I- think it's the same bird," answered Tom, "But he didn't bring me anything, and I hope he never does!"

"He is just being friendly. If we are smart, we will take his advice and get up to start the new day," roared Joe, as he started getting dressed.

The men sat up and slowly started pulling on their boots.

Tom brought fresh water from the stream, so all the men could wash. With many shivers and mumbled words, the men were finally washed, dressed, and raring to go. "Mushroom porridge is ready. Bring your bowls and your appetites!" yelled Tom, as he twirled around the ladled. "We will also have some wild berries to eat with our porridge this morning. When I went for water, I found these berries growing near the stream's bank."

The men ate well; in fact, they didn't leave one berry behind them.

"All right, men, we must be moving on," signaled Zip, as he pulled on his knap-sack.

The men washed out their dishes, packed them into their knap-sacks and were soon off once more.

The weather remained mild, but a light drizzle sifted through the overhead tree branches. The men pulled their collars up and their hats down and kept on walking.

"How many miles long is this forest?" asked Ben, "It seems like we covered more than fifteen miles already."

"I am not sure how far we must walk till we reach the end of the forest. No one from our world has ever walked to the end of the forest. The map states twenty miles, but that may not be accurate. We have many more days to go before we see the bright sky again. Since we live under the mountain, I kind of like looking up and seeing trees instead of the hot sun," responded Zip, while staring at the trees.

So, on they pressed, cautiously walking around exposed tree roots, scrambling over small rocks and skirting puddles.

Mushrooms of all colors, red and pink, violet, white, round and strong, small and fragile shapes grew in this forest as well as wild violets, beautiful white Indian pipes and lovely flowering myrtle. Zip had seen some of these wonders before, but Ben, Zith, Chris, Tom and Joe never had. They were intrigued by all the colors and shapes and the dainty aroma of the violets. Now and then, one of the men would stop to smell a flower and would smile with delight.

"All these mushrooms are pretty," Zip forewarned, "But don't be fooled by their beauty. Some of these mushrooms are poisonous. Don't eat any that you are not familiar with."

Tom picked a miniature violet and tucked it in his buttonhole, straightened his jacket and walked proudly on.

"Ouch!" Zith shrieked.

The men rotated around to find Zith dancing up and down on one foot, while holding his other foot in his hand.

"What happened?" Joe asked, with concern showing on his face, "Did you hurt your foot?"

"Of course, I hurt my foot. Do you think I would be jumping up and down on one foot, while holding my other foot if I did not hurt my foot?" screamed Zith.

"Let's not get excited, men," Zip motioned, "Sit down, Zith, and let me look at your foot."

The men helped Zith to a flat rock and sat him down.

"Take your boot off, Zith, so I can see what is bothering you."

"Let us help with your boot," suggested Tom and Ben.

The two men gently pulled the boot off. They then stood back for Zip's inspection of Zith's injured foot.

"Seems like you stepped on a sharp rock, Zith, and it went right through your boot because your foot has a wound in it. It is bleeding, so we will have to wash it out," Zip reached for his knap-sack and took out a bowl.

"While Joe and I fetch some water, Tom can build a fire. Then we can really clean out the wound," Ben said.

The men set about their appointed duties, leaving Zith and Zip sitting on the low, flat rock.

"We will camp here tonight, Zith, to give your foot a chance to rest. In the morning, we will see what the story is," announced Zip, as he patted Zith on the shoulder.

When Ben and Joe returned with the water, Tom poured some into a pot and placed it over the fire. After the water boiled, he took the pot away from the fire. When it cooled enough to be used, Zip cleaned Zith's wound. Zith did not say anything, but his face became pale and showed the pain he experienced from the treatment.

"There," said Zip, "If an infection does not set in you will be up and around soon. I am sure some of Tom's delicious soup and hearty greens will be good medicine for you."

Zith settled back on a bed of leaves the men arranged for him. After supper, he fell asleep.

Zip called the men away from Zith.

"Men, can you hear me, I am talking in a whisper so as not to awaken Zith. His foot does not look very good. The wound was deeper than I first thought. I don't feel he can walk too far for a few days. We have two choices: we can wait for him to recover, or some of us can continue and the rest can stay with Zith, then catch up later with us. What do you say, men?"

Tom spoke first. "I will stay here with Zith and cook for him until he is well. Then we can follow you."

"Good," proclaimed Zip with a smile, "I don't like to leave you, but I feel it would be best. We will sneak out in the morning before Zith wakes up. If he were awake he would want to keep going, wound or no wound."

"Let's get to sleep now so we can be refreshed in the morning," announced Ben."

One by one, the men fell asleep.

Tom started to snore. His lip moved up and down as he snored.

Off to the side of the campsite, a small, dark shadow appeared. It crept closer to Tom. Its large ears shook, and its nose twitched. It quietly climbed onto Tom's leg and wobbled up towards Tom's snoring mouth. As it touched Tom's face, Tom knocked it off, but never woke up. Next, it walked over to Joe. Slowly, it walked up Joe's arm and settled on his chest, looking down at the sleeping man. Joe woke up and screamed, waking up all the other men. Joe jumped up and danced around as he yelled that a monster was on him. Zip carefully searched for the monster and found a cute, little, brown mouse shivering in the grass near the campsite.

"I found your monster, Joe, and it really looks mean," laughed Zip.

The men crowded around the mouse, whose wide eyes and tiny face registered terror, and now it was time for the mouse to be scared! But, then the mouse saw they meant no harm and he ran away.

THE PARTY SPLITS UP

CHAPTER 6

As dawn approached, Tom awakened Chris, Ben, Joe and Zip. Noiselessly, they dressed and ate breakfast of porridge and berries. They did not light a fire so as not to awaken Zith.

"Do not worry about us," whispered Tom, "I will take good care of Zith, and we will follow you in a few days' time."

"Fine, Tom, but remember to keep close watch on Zith's wound. We did not bring any medicine with us, even though we thought we remembered everything," Zip said sadly.

The friends said their good-farewells. With Zip leading the way, the remaining robust travelers trudged farther into the forest.

Tom went to the stream, where he filled his pot with water. Then, he collected more red, juicy berries, was chased by a bee in the berry patch, some wild vegetables and walked back to camp.

Zith was just beginning to stir when Tom arrived. Zith yawned and rolled over.

"How are you feeling?" asked Tom.

"I am too sleepy to tell. Give me a few minutes to wake up, then I can answer you better," Zith said wearily.

Tom started to build a fire. He had set a stick horizontally across the tops of two vertically standing sticks and hung a pot from this horizontal stick. The fire soon roared under the pot, and Tom began to make breakfast.

A few minutes later, Zith, fully awake now, sat up.

"Where are the others?" he asked.

"Oh, they went on ahead. We will follow them as soon as your foot feels better," Tom said breezily while waving his hand in the air.

"I could have gone on. They did not have to leave us here. I am strong enough, and besides this is only a scratch," yelled Zith. As he spoke, Zith tried to stand up. From the expression on his face, Tom knew Zith's foot really hurt.

"Take it easy, Zith. I'm not a doctor, but I think I can help you. Then you will be well, and we can go together to meet our friends," Tom chortled cheerfully.

"I cooked leafy, green, vegetable soup for you. Eat it up, for it will give you some strength. Here, have this cupful; it is not too hot." Tom extended the cup to Zith.

"You wanted to go with the others to retrieve our violin, and now you are stuck with me. It is not fair for you," cried Zith.

"I would not have it any other way. Now eat all your soup, and let us not hear any more about it," pleaded Tom.

Zith finished the soup and settled down again. As Tom cleaned the dishes, Zith drifted off once more to sleep.

"He sure does not look like himself to me," thought Tom, as he looked down at the sleeping Zith, "I am glad I stayed with him."

Tom's concern seemed justified, for Zith slept the rest of the morning and into the late afternoon.

A worried look crossed Tom's face when he placed his hand upon Zith's forehead.

"He is running a temperature," whispered Tom, "Whatever will I do for him?"

Overhead, high up on a branch, cawed Mr. Bluejay as if trying to tell Tom something. Tom, worried about Zith, did not look up or acknowledge his friend, Mr. Bluejay.

When Zith opened his eyes, Tom sat there next to him with a cool cup of water.

"Drink this, Zith, it will help you feel a little cooler. You are running a temperature. Does your head hurt you?" inquired Tom.

"Yes, it feels like a ton of rocks has landed on my head," answered Zith, with his hands cradling his head.

"Will you eat some nice, cool berries now? I placed them in a cup of cold water. They are superb," coaxed Tom.

Zith ate a few berries, but could not eat any more; he just felt too sick. Tom inspected Zith's foot and found it had turned a reddish color around the wound.

"Oh, moley oh, whatever will I do for Zith? He is so sick, and I do not know what I can do for him," cried Tom.

Just then, Mr. Bluejay swooped down from the tree and stood near Tom. Tom turned pale when he noticed the bird because Tom thought Mr. Bluejay had come to eat him up.

"Caw, caw," sang Mr. Bluejay, as he inched closer to Tom.

"If you plan on eating me, Mr. Bluejay, do it now or leave me alone. I am too worried about Zith to care," said Tom.

Mr. Bluejay came closer and placed his beak on Tom's shoulder. Tom realized Mr. Bluejay wanted to be friends and wanted to help him.

"Thanks, Mr. Bluejay, but what can you do to help? You do not have any medicine. Oh, if only I could fly like you. I could fly back to the cave for help, but I must face the truth, I cannot fly," said Tom.

Mr. Bluejay flew up into the air, then returned to Tom. He did this five times. Finally, Tom said, "Are you trying to tell me something, Mr. Bluejay?"

Mr. Bluejay cawed.

"It seems like you want to go for help for Zith. That is very nice of you, but you cannot speak to tell them what is wrong. I can speak, but I cannot fly. Oh, moley oh, what shall I do," groaned Tom.

Mr. Bluejay once more flew up into the air and returned to Tom.

"What are you saying, Mr. Bluejay? Are you offering me a ride? What if I fall off? Then, no one will know about Zith, and he will be sicker. However, if I remain here without medicine, he will get worse," said Tom.

Mr. Bluejay came around in front of Tom and stood there.

"Very well," said Tom, "But let me check Zith first."

Tom placed a blanket on Zith and felt his head once more. "Yes, he is really sick. I must go for help. If this be the end of me that is too bad, but I must try to help Zith."

"Ok, friend, I will try my best to get help, and to safely return back to you." After saying this, Tom decided to climbed upon Mr. Bluejay's back and they were off.

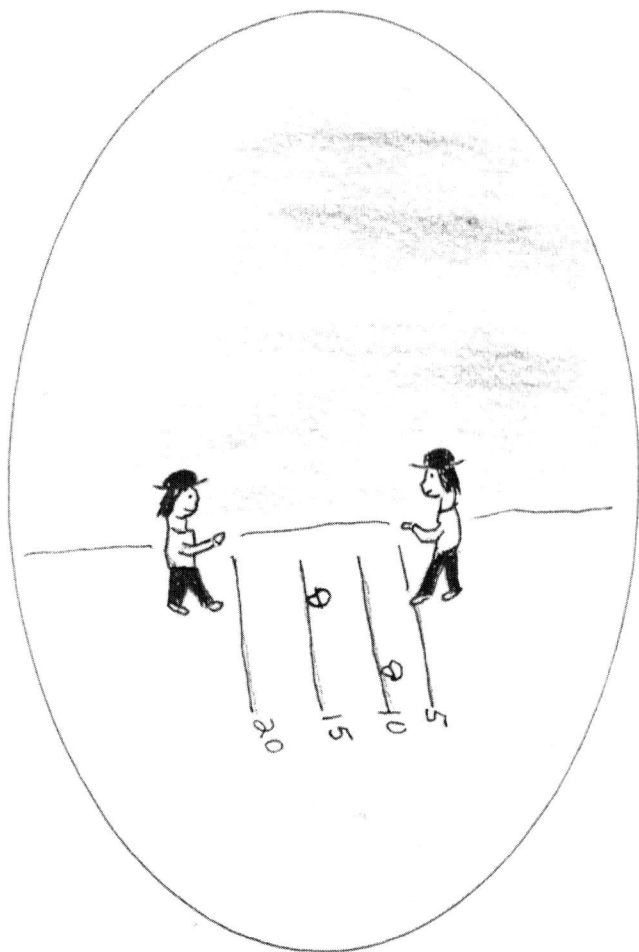

BACK AT THE CAVE

CHAPTER 7

The morning dawned bright and clear as the Wee Cave Men continued on their journey. However, at the same time Tom was flying on the back of Mr. Bluejay to the cave.

Back at the cave, Belle sat brushing her long blonde hair in front of her mirror and thought about Zip. She thought how brave he was to lead this great undertaking and how handsome he looked when he left the cave.

"Oh, mother, do you think Zip will return safely? Do you think anything terrible will happen to him?" cried Belle.

"We can only wait and see. What will be will be," answered Pat, as she placed her hand onto Belle's shoulder.

From outside Belle's chamber, two children's voices could be heard.

"Let's play toss the mushroom!" yelled Danny, as he tossed a mushroom up and down in his hand.

"Yes, I would like that," laughed Fred as he ran over to Danny.

The two five year old friends relished playing this game. They drew lines a few feet away from where they stood. Each line was a foot past the last line, and there were four lines altogether. One boy stands on a designated spot and tosses a mushroom toward the four lines.   As the mushroom lands on the line or just touches the line, the amount is counted.

Each line had a score, the first line was worth 5 points, the second line was 10 points, the third line was 15 points and the fourth line was 20 points. The boys have four chances each, then their four tosses are added up for a total amount of points each round. 100 points wins the game, if the mushroom does not touch the line, no score is given for that turn.

"I will be first." Danny tossed the mushroom, which bounced on the ground, rolled over the first line and came to a stop between the first and second lines.

"Try again Danny, "yelled Fred excitedly, stepping from foot to foot, "You still have three more chances."

Danny's next toss placed the mushroom right across the second line.

"That is 10 points for me," yelled Danny, "Write it down, so we will not forget. Here comes my third toss. Good! Five more points!"

"By golly, all that noise is hurting my ears. I can't even think straight," roared a voice from a small chamber, farther down the corridor. The chamber belongs to Bill, who loves his privacy. When Bill heard the boys playing, he closed his curtains to try to keep out their voices.

However, another chamber off this long winding corridor belonged to Peter and Pat.

"Do you think the men will come back safely, Peter?" asked Pat, who had just returned from her daughter Belle's room."

"I hope to see them all safe and well once more. We do not know what dangers they are facing now; let's hope they are well," answered Peter.

"It will break Belle's heart if anything bad should happen to Zip," whispered Pat, with a worried look on her face.

"Come Pat, let's go into the dining hall for some refreshments," said Peter. Extending his arm, he led Pat out of their chamber and into the long corridor. As they left their quiet chamber to walk down the corridor, they could hear Danny and Fred still playing their game. They smiled at each other, for the excited voices of youth brought back memories of when Belle was a child.

When they reached the dining hall, a sense of anxiety hung in the air. As he sat down, Peter looked from one face to another. Finally, he asked, "Is something wrong?" When no one answered, he said, "If we have not heard any bad news, let us assume all is well, and soon our men will return safely carrying our violin. What say you?"

"Let's believe the best!" cried Casey, jumping off her chair with excitement.

Suddenly, the atmosphere changed and once again people talked to and smiled at each other.

"We must have hope!" shouted Peter, while standing tall by Pat's side, "Without hope, there is nothing."

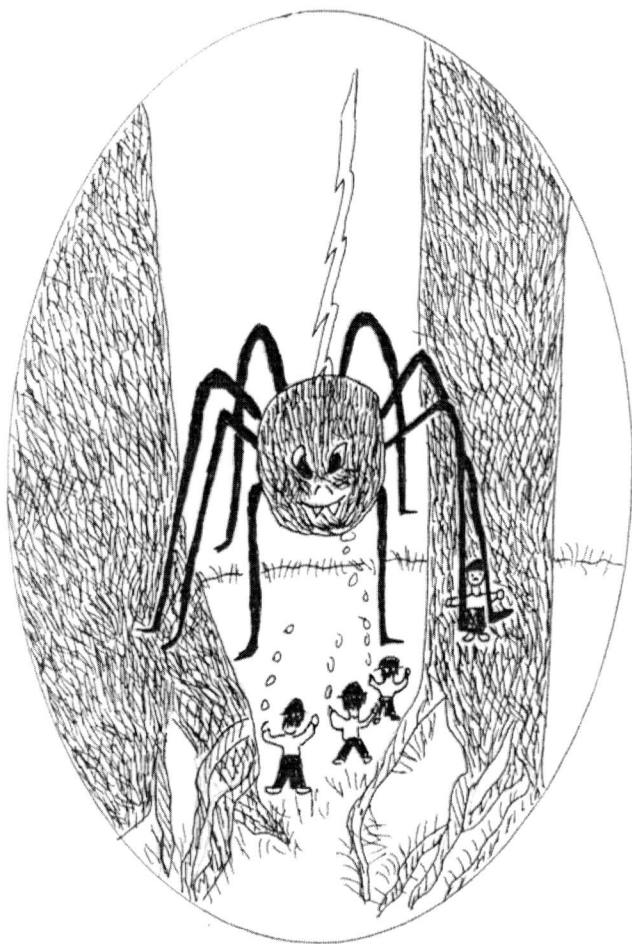

RETURNING TO ZIP AND THE MEN

CHAPTER 8

"When can we stop for a rest Zip? We have been walking since daybreak," Ben wearily asked.

"I guess this is as good a time as any," replied Zip. "Let us sit down and rest a bit."

"My coffee-making is not the greatest," ventured Chris, as he smiled at the others, "Will anyone here make us a good pot of coffee?"

"I would be glad to try," offered Joe, "Do not expect too much from me. I have not made coffee in a long time. By crackers, I think anyone's coffee would be an improvement over Chris' coffee."

"We will see about that," smiled Chris.

The men made themselves as comfortable as possible.

"I hope Zith is feeling better," said Ben, as he stretched out on the ground. "Do you think he is, Zip?"

"That was a nasty cut on his foot. By now, he is either feeling much better, and we will see him and Tom shortly, or he is much worse. I hope we will see him shortly," said Zip, with a worried look on his face.

"Are we nearing the end of the forest yet, Zip? These trees are so tall and their branches are so leafy that I will be sorry to leave them," sighed Chris.

Pulling out his map, Zip traced a line with his finger.

"We are almost at the end of the forest, or at least at the end of this map. Remember, we do not know what is at the end of the forest. Our map only goes to this point. It will be up to us to finish this map. We must be brave and hope for the best," replied Zip.

"Let us sing while we enjoy our coffee," said Joe, standing up and waving his hands to conduct their singing. "I think this coffee came out great!"

"Well, not great," teased Chris, "But, it is better than mine."

The men sang:

"Although we left our friends behind
It will not be forever,
Some day soon we will return
For our bonds we did not sever.

Glad we will be to see again
Our wives and children too,
But we had to make this journey
To our conscience we must be true."

As the men settled back with their coffee, Joe made them some leafwiches.

"Here, Ben have a leafwich," said Joe.

"A what?" Ben asked with a frown on his face.

"By crackers, I said a leafwich!," yelled Joe, in a loud clear voice.

"I heard what you said," smiled Ben, "But what is a leafwich?"

"A leafwich is two pieces of lettuce, one on top and one on the bottom with a filling inside. Today, the filling is mushroom mash. Now do you know what a leafwich is?" Joe demanded.

"Sure," laughed Ben, "If you say so."

The men laughed as they ate their leafwiches. They had to agree the food tasted good.

"We still have more land to cover before we settle in for the night, so do not take too long for lunch," warned Zip.

The men pulled their jacket collars up around their necks for the wind chill cut them as icy swords. Leaves swirled around them, while the branches swayed and rocked up and down vigorously. Then, thunder cracked and lightning flashed, causing the men to huddle closer together where they sat beneath the trees. The branches resembled long, skinny arms reaching out to grab them.

"I hope the lightning does not hit these trees," Chris uttered nervously as he looked toward the trees, "They are so big, I would hate to think of them falling onto us."

"By crackers, where did this storm come from? It was so quiet a few minutes ago," Joe shouted, as he held his ears.

"I heard the makers of this map ran into such a storm. They feared for their lives and made their way back to the mountain without completing this map. Are we to be like them, or shall we continue on our way?" screamed Zip.

The men looked at each other, then Ben offered, "We said we would retrieve our violin, and I think we should go on and do so."

"We cannot let a little rain and noise end our journey." complained Chris.

"Let us move on then!" bellowed Zip, trying to be heard over the thunder.

Just then, a black, furry body supported by long, spindly legs appeared from out of the shadows. It was a monstrous spider with gleaming brown eyes. As the arachnid bore down upon them, the men froze with terror. Suddenly, the spider moved faster and jumped on Joe, who shrieked and grew pale. The spider held Joe within its eight legs. Joe looked as though he were in jail.

Zip roared, "We must save Joe! Hurry, there may be more of these creatures!"

"What can we do?" cried Chris, shivering in his boots.

"Pick up some rocks and throw them at the beast. Aim carefully. Do not strike Joe!" shrieked Zip, "Throw on the count of three. Ready, one...two...three!"

One by one, the men hit the spider with the rocks. Lightning flashed and thunder clapped; the spider reared up and waved his arms madly. Then he shook his body to shake off the falling raining.

"Once again, men,! Zip picked up another rock.

The spider raised a front leg to try to grab Zip.

"Oh no, you don't!" Zip, slammed the rock at the spider's head. "One prisoner is enough at a time! More rocks, men!"

Then as the next round of rocks were hurled, the spider suddenly jumped backwards, releasing his captive. Joe, fell to the ground trembling from head to toe.

The spider opened his mouth to show his sharp, pointed, teeth. Just then, lightning cracked and struck the spider on his front, menacing tooth. The spider stepped backward and groaned.

Ben threw a rock, which hit the spider in the mouth. The spider moaned and pulled back. Then he turned around and moved back into the shadows.

The men ran to Joe.

"Are you all right, Joe?" gasped Chris.

"I-I-think so. What was that thing?" whispered Joe, in a low faint voice.

"The largest spider I ever saw," stated Zip, as he swallowed hard. "Let us hurry away from this place. I would not like to meet his friends!"

The men helped Joe onto his feet, packed up their things and once more started on their way. They found their footing very difficult now. Everything that once was solid earth had now turned to mud. Their boots oozed with the brown, mushy earth.

"Hold hands and form a line as we walk," urged Zip, "Then we will not be separated."

Linking hands the men formed a line, not a straight line to be sure, as they fought the gusty winds with each new step.

49

BACK TO ZITH

CHAPTER 9

As Zip and the other men fought their way through the furious storm, Zith lay on the bed of leaves, under the trees, where Tom had left him. The full canopy of tree branches blocked out much of the storm, but a steady trickle of raindrops found their way through the leaves to hit Zith on the head. For awhile, Zith didn't notice the raindrops, as he continued to sleep. A few minutes passed before Zith opened his eyes.

"Tom, where are you?" he cried, "Seems like a storm is brewing."

Zith sat up and looked around. His head felt light, as the forest spun about him.

"Tom, are you here?"

Just then, a raindrop hit the campfire and sizzled amid the flames.

What is that? Is someone there? Oh, it is just the fire," sighed Zith, as he held his head. Tom must be busy doing something somewhere else, so I will just move myself out of the raindrops' path and try to keep dry," Zith said to himself.

As Zith tried to stand up, the sharp pain in his foot reminded him of his wound.

"Jingo, I forgot about my foot. I better have a look at it." Zith pulled off his sock.

"Let's see. It is not as red as it was before. It is still a bit swollen though. My temperature is not too high right now, so maybe my foot is healing. I will put my sock back on and my boots and look for a drier spot to wait for Tom." exclaimed Zith, as his eyes looked around the area.

"I cannot stand up very well, so I will need a crutch to support me. This sapling will do. I just have enough string in my pocket to tie the branches together to form my crutch. Jingo, just enough. Now I must try it out. Well, here goes." Zith slowly lifted himself up and, with the aid of his crutch, could take his weight off his injured foot.

"I am a bit dizzy now, but I must fight this weak feeling until I am safely in a dry spot," thought Zith.

He glanced around to establish which way to go. As his eyes swept the forest, they fell upon a tree hollowed out by squirrels, which now stood unoccupied. Limping over to the tree, Zith peered inside.

"Very dark in here. I must build a fire right outside this tree. The light from the fire will show me just what is in this hole. I will need some twigs and dry grass and a little luck, so the storm does not get worse here and wash out my fire," Zith thought.

When the smoke had cleared and the fire burned brightly, Zith looked into the hollowed out tree.

"It is not particularly fancy, but it will be my home until I am well again," said Zith aloud.

Gingerly, Zith climbed into the tree and settled himself down to rest. The tree felt warm and cozy. Best of all, it was nice and dry.

"Tom will find me when he returns," thought Zith, "Tom will see my fire and find me here. I must sleep now to save my strength-I-am-very-tired."

With the fire blazing, Zith yawned and soon fell asleep.

TOM AND MR. BLUEJAY'S TRIP

CHAPTER 10

"It is very windy up here, Mr. Bluejay. I hope I do not fall off," whispered Tom. Now the trees looked small to Tom, as he and Mr. Bluejay flew over the forest. Tom shuddered with fear.

"If I fall, Mr. Bluejay, catch me with your beak, as I am not too heavy," pleaded Tom.

The bluejay flew on with one thought in mind, to get Tom to the cave.

I hope Zip is still asleep," said Tom. "Do you hear me, Mr. Bluejay? Your wings are flapping up and down and the wind rushing around us is making so much noise that I cannot think straight. Fly fast, Mr. Bluejay. We must help Zith."

So on they traveled over high tree and low, over stream and pond, winging their way toward the cave.

"Fly to the beginning of the forest, Mr. Bluejay, then I will tell you the way from that point to the mouth of the cave," shrieked Tom.

Tom pulled his hat down over his ears. The wind blew into his eyes, so he had to close them almost completely.

"I hope Zith is feeling better now. I did not like to leave him, but I did not have a choice," thought Tom.

While flying over the treetops, Tom opened his eyes a little and turned his face over his shoulder, out of the path of the oncoming wind. For the first time, he noticed more bluejays than he had ever seen before. They perched in among the branches as if they were waiting for something exciting to happen.

"Are these birds your friends, Mr. Bluejay? They are cawing at us as we pass."

Just then, Tom's boot slipped off and hurtled toward the forest floor. Mr. Bluejay cawed loudly and a smaller bluejay, from the top tree branch, intercepted the falling boot before it hit the ground. He then flew up to Tom and passed the boot from his beak to the wee man's hand.

"Oh, thank you friend. I thought I had lost my boot forever. I cannot put it on while I am up on Mr. Bluejay's back, so I will hold it in my right hand and hold Mr. Bluejay with my left hand. My bootless foot is getting cold up here. Would you mind if I tuck my foot into and under some of your nice warm feathers, Mr. Bluejay?" Tom pleaded.

Mr. Bluejay cawed his consent.

"My wife, Flo, would really be shocked if she could see me now. She would never believe I would fly up here near the clouds," Tom revealed happily.

"Speaking of clouds, I think these clouds are getting darker. They were white when we left Zith, but now they are dark. I hope Zith is not getting wet. Oh, moley oh, let us hurry, Mr. Bluejay. We must help Zith, he trusts me to help him. I must come back to him."

"I hope Zip and the other men are making good progress. If I make it to the cave and back to Zith safely, I will have a lot of traveling to do to catch up with them," thought Tom.

So on they flew, safe in their good intentions of bringing aid to Zith.

DESTINATION REACHED

CHAPTER 11

On they flew, one mission in mind, one place to land.

"Keep going, Mr. Bluejay, we are almost there. There cannot be many more miles to fly. I am glad we met your friends. They are flying with us. See, look behind," said Tom excitedly, while turning his head around.

Mr. Bluejay turned his head around, and Tom thought he noticed Mr. Bluejay smile when he saw his friends. There they were, a squadron of bluejays, flying in formation over the trees.

Just then, Mr. Bluejay flew out of the forest into a clearing.

"Continue flying to the side of that mountain; we have made it home. Oh, moley oh, I never thought we would get here safely. Fly up to the top of the path. That's right, Mr. Bluejay, now land on the path," said Tom, as he sighed with relief.

Tom scrambled down from Mr. Bluejay's back and sat on the grass to pull his boot on.

Just then, a familiar voice rang out. "Tom, is that you? Where are the others? Why did you ride upon the bluejay's back?"

"Why, Sam, it is really good to see you again! Come over here and meet my friend. Do not be afraid; he will not hurt you," coaxed Tom.

Cautiously, Sam approached Tom.

Tom introduced Sam to Mr. Bluejay.

"How do you do, Mr. Bluejay?" Sam, shyly said, as he backed-up. Sam had never been so close to a bird before.

Mr. Bluejay cawed.

"Now, Sam, I will come into the cave and tell you all about my journey. Mr. Bluejay, will you wait for me? I must return to Zith." pleaded Tom, with concern in his eyes.

Mr. Bluejay placed his beak on Tom's shoulder, and Tom knew Mr. Bluejay would not leave without him. Tom placed his arm around Sam's shoulder, as they walked into the cave.

Once inside the cave, Tom felt secure again. His step became springier and his heart felt lighter. He stopped for a sweater, in the little sweater chamber, and then continued down the tunnel to the main dining room. As Tom walked into the dining room everything became quiet. Everyone stopped talking and walking to look at Tom.

Flo looked up from her mending and saw Tom. A wide smile covered her face and she ran to meet him.

"Oh, Tom, we have been waiting and worrying for you and the others. Are you all right?" She threw herself into Tom's arms and hugged him.

"Yes, dear, I am fine. I returned alone. I must talk to Peter to arrange the details for my return trip." Tom tried to explain.

"Your return trip? Must you leave again?" A worried looked appeared on Flo's face.

"I am afraid I must." said Tom, as he walked toward the door.

"Tom, it is good to see you," Peter spoke, as he walked into the room. "But, where are the others?"

"Let us sit down, and I will tell you everything." replied Tom, as he dropped onto a chair.

"I will get you some mushroom tea. It will calm your nerves." said Flo.

Belle came into the room and sat near her father.

As quickly as he could, Tom related the journey to Peter and the others. He told them about Zith's cut foot and about how he had to leave his patient to summon help.

"How is Zip?" inquired Belle, as she looked up from the chair.

"The last time I saw Zip he was very well. The others continued the expedition," answered Tom, "but I had to return to the cave."

"Poor Zith," said Peter, "We must bring medicine to him, so he will be well again. Are you willing, Tom, to leave again with us to show us the way?"

"Yes, of course, I will, but first I must check with Mr. Bluejay. If it were not for Mr. Bluejay, I never would have reached home," answered Tom.

When Tom emerged from the cave, he received a surprise. Standing outside the cave entrance with Mr. Bluejay were twelve other bluejays.

Tom walked over to Mr. Bluejay. "Are you and your friends going back the way we came, Mr. Bluejay? We really could use a ride to bring medicine back to Zith," Tom said, while he held his breathe for the answer.

Mr. Bluejay cawed. Then, the twelve other bluejays cawed. Tom smiled and returned to the cave.

"Peter, you and eleven men can return with me to Zith. Mr. Bluejay has strong friends, and they will gladly fly us there," announced Tom.

"I will feed the birds, so they will have enough energy for the flight," said Peter, while throwing seeds and fruits on the ground. "Meanwhile, Tom, you round up the other eleven men, but do not forget to pack the medicine."

"Very well," said Tom, hurrying to herd the birds together, as Peter left the room. "Any man who is willing to come on this dangerous journey, please step over here. Twelve bluejays have offered us their help. We do not need twelve men, but if twelve men want to come, we will be pleased to have them along for the ride."

After Peter finished feeding the birds, he returned to the dining room. There, he found the new group of men waiting to aid their friends.

Belle put food into their bags, and Pat filled up their jugs.

"Step up, and give your name," Tom ordered.

The eleven men who stepped forward and called out their names were Ted, a little fellow, 4" tall, David, slightly taller at 4 ½" tall, sporting a brown beard, John, wearing a cap over his blond hair, standing 3 ½", Jerry, dressed in blue, stood 3" tall, Ned, with his tiny eye glasses, on the end of his nose, is 5" tall, Sal, with his tubby body, stands 4" tall, Jimmy, wearing green pants and brown jacket, stands 5" tall, Bert, always with a twinkle in his blue eyes, is 5 ½" tall, George, a very quiet, studious fellow, stands 4 ½," Matt, lean and wiry, 4" tall, and Scott, a witty, jolly soul, standing 4" tall.

"We will leave within the hour, men. Eat and make ready. We must reach Zith in time," announced, Tom, while making sure the medicine is packed.

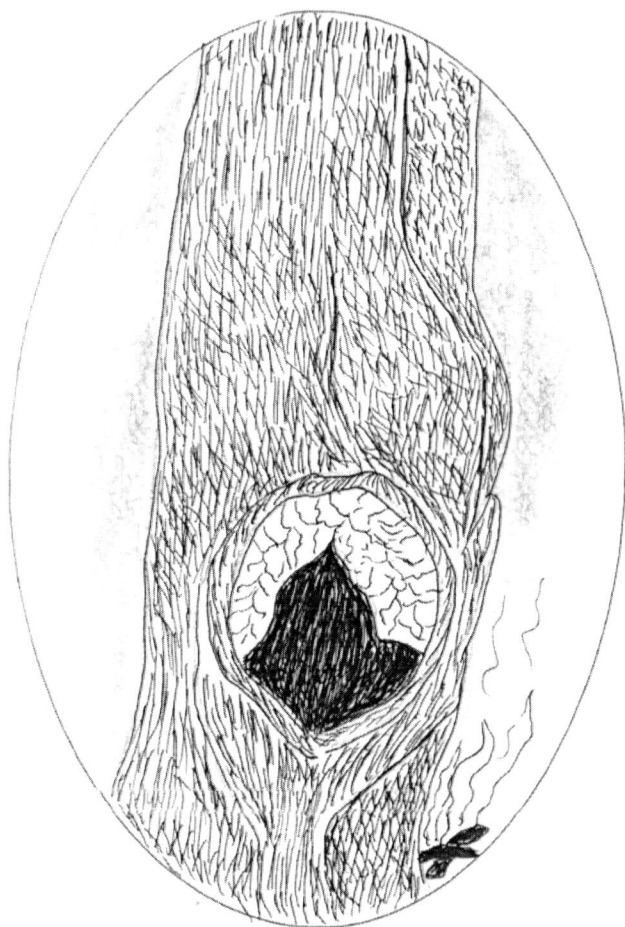

HELP FOR ZITH

CHAPTER 12

After the men finished eating, they gathered up their bags and jugs before lining up for inspection.

"It will not be an easy journey. We must fly on the bluejays' backs, up where it is cold and windy, for a rather long time. Do you all agree to accept whatever may happen?" asked Peter.

"We do," chorused the men.

"Then let us depart to aid Zith." Tom excitedly move forward.

The men said their good-byes to the remaining community and walked up the tunnel out into the bright sunshine.

"It is clear and sunny here," said Tom, spreading his arms out wide, "But it was not so when I left Zith. Let us hope the weather has cleared up there."

"Mr. Bluejay, I will ride on your back, if it is all right with you. Please ask your friends to form a line, so the other men can climb aboard their backs," Tom signaled with his hand.

Bluejay cawed to the other birds, who all lined up. The men looked at the birds, swallowed hard and climbed aboard.

"Hold on tightly, men. We do not want to lose anyone!" shouted Tom, through cupped hands.

"Are we ready to start on our trip, men?" asked Peter.

"We are!" The men spoke as one.

Belle walked over to Peter and blew him a kiss. "Please be careful, Father. Return in good health."

"I will be fine, child. Your job while I am gone is to help your mother cheer up the others. Their spirits must stay high, for we have had enough long faces in our world," answered Peter, with a warm smile.

"All right, Mr. Bluejay, we are ready to leave. Fly, fly high and speedily. Fly over trees and streams; fly us to Zith's side. We must hurry if we hope to save Zith. So be off!" yelled Tom, tapping Mr. Bluejay's side.

Mr. Bluejay ran a little, fluttered his wings and lifted off the ground. The remaining birds did the same, until all the birds soared above the earth.

Belle waved her scarf to her father and the others, then walked back into the cave.

The birds flew over the hill and back toward the forest. They floated on the air currents, while the men held on tightly. Some of the men closed their eyes because they were up so high, they did not want to look down. Others loved to look down at the wonderful sights below them, while the rest had one eye open and one eye closed.

The birds flew in formation. Tom and Mr. Bluejay flew in the lead position. Tom looked back over his shoulder to check on the men. All moved along as planned. The men had different expressions on their faces; some were frightened, while others showed intensity of the mission. Tom remembered dropping his boot on the last trip, so he curled up his toes to make sure his boots stayed on this time.

They flew on. The weather remained fair, but not as sunny as it had been near the cave.

"Mr. Bluejay, I hope you remember the exact location where we left Zith. From this high up, everything looks the same to me. Oh, moley oh, we must find Zith!" cried Tom, straining his eyes to see the forest ground.

Bluejay cawed to reassure Tom. Then suddenly, Bluejay cawed what appeared to Tom to be a signal, and all the birds started to descend.

They landed in an open patch of forest floor. After the birds landed, the men remained on board until they were sure they had landed safely. Then, one by one they climbed off and dropped their bags and jugs on the ground.

"We have had a safe journey, and I thank Mr. Bluejay and his friends for that, but now we must find Zith. He does not appear to be here, although this is the spot where I left him. This was our campsite and our cooking pot," said Tom, anxiously. "Help me find Zith, men; he could not have gone far."

The men spread out and started to search. Tom and Peter stayed together. As they walked around the old campsite, Peter noticed a young tree nearby had been chopped down. Tom and Peter followed a trail of footprints and strange marks that led away from the campsite. After the rain, the ground was muddy and Zith, unwittingly, left a trail behind.

"The tracks go off in this direction," fluttered Tom, turning his head around.

"Look over there. There is a fire burning beside this tree," pointed, Peter, gesturing towards the tree.

The two men walked over to the tree.

"This tree has a hole in its side. Look into the hole, then tell me if you see anything," whispered Peter, suspiciously.

After skirting the fire, Tom peered into the tree.

"Zith, Zith is that you? Wake up, Zith it is I, Tom. I have returned with help for you."

"What, who is there?" Zith sounded half-asleep. "Tom, is that you?"

"Yes, Zith. I brought Peter and eleven other men with me," said Tom, with a big grin on his face, "We have medicine for you. Climb out of this tree so we can see your foot."

Peter called the others to ease Zith, crutch and all, out of the tree.

"Oh, that was what made the strange marks next to your footprints," sighed Tom, with a broad smile.

"My foot is not as bad now, Tom. It took a few days to heal, but it feels better now. My fever broke the day after you left. Since then, I have been feeling a bit better. I still feel a little weak, but otherwise improved," said Zith, wiggling his foot in the air.

"George has some clean bandages and medicine for you, Zith. After he administers to you, we will eat," announced an elated, Peter.

"I will prepare a good meal for us in celebration of Zith's return to good health!" cried Tom, as he gleefully grabbed his pots and pans.

"Allow me to help you, Tom," said Bert, "I'm good at assisting, I also like to cook."

"Good, I can use your help," replied Tom, happily, while handing Bert a pot. "Let us make the best feast we can under these conditions."

"The rest of you men sit down and relax. We will serve dinner soon," announced Tom, who hurried off with Bert to fulfill their promise.

BLUEJAY AND HIS FRIENDS

CHAPTER 13

Tom and Bert busied themselves preparing the meal, to try to make it as special as they could, in hopes the men would calm down and relieve their tension.

Zith rested against a tree. Next to him sat Peter. The other men sat in small groups and talked about their wonderful flight adventure. "I was a little frightened," admitted Peter, "I never was up so high!"

"The bluejay I rode on was a lovely young lady. She was very kind and delivered me safely back to earth," smiled George, with a dreamy look in his eye.

"This adventure has just started, but I am finding it a great experience," Matt, exclaimed, hitting himself on the knee.

Meanwhile, Bluejay and his friends perched in the tree above the men. They too were resting after the long flight. The birds cawed lowly to each other. Now and then, a bluejay reached back with her beak and preened her tail feathers or her wing feathers.

"Mr. Bluejay, do not go away. I am cooking enough food for you and your friends to eat with us," called Tom, "We really appreciate what you did for us. We will always be your friends."

Down flew Bluejay to the ground, where he hopped over to Tom, and placed his beak upon Tom's shoulder.

"You will be my friend forever, Mr. Bluejay. Is that what you mean?" asked Tom.

Bluejay cawed. Tom smiled warmly at his friend.

"Come and eat men. Mr. Bluejay, please call your friends to supper. Birds over here and men over there," directed Tom.

In a few minutes, the men and their feathered friends were eating and enjoying one another's company. The birds cawed as the men talked, adding to the festive mood their closeness created.

"So Zith, tell me just how you feel. When will you be strong enough to start home?" asked Peter.

"Start home?" screeched Zith, sitting up straight as an arrow, "Surely you jest with me. I started out to retrieve our violin, and in a day or so, I plan on continuing my mission."

"Are you sure you are well enough to continue this difficult journey?" soothed Peter, as he touched Zith's arm.

"I am sure. Even if I get sick again, our friends the bluejays will help us. So you see, there is no need to worry about it," summed up Zith, with confidence registering over his face.

The birds turned their heads and cawed.

"Very well, Zith, if that is what you want. We will rest for another day, then continue on our way," declared Peter.

Just then, Bluejay and his friends flew off. The men wondered where they were going in such a hurry.

A few minutes later, the bluejays returned. In their beaks, they carried berry branches, which they placed in a pile before Tom's feet.

"Why, thank you, Mr. Bluejay. It is so nice of you to bring us some dessert. I will wash these berries and divide them up for all of us to eat. It is good to have you as a friend," Tom petted the leg of Mr. Bluejay and smiled up at him.

Then, Bluejay and his friends flew off, but the men knew if they needed them, the birds would be back.

The men ate the sweet berries, as they watched the bluejays disappear into the sky.

ZIP AND THE MEN COME INTO
THE CLEARING

CHAPTER 14

"Keep walking, men and hold each other's hands tightly! We must stay together!" shouted Zip above the noise of the storm.

SPLASH!

"Oops!" cried Ben, as he fell into the mud, covering his red hair with brown, mushy goo.

"What happened, Ben?" asks Zip, standing with his hands on his hips.

"I slipped on a rock. That rock moved as I stepped on it." Ben replied slowly, looking down at the rock.

"Crackers, now I have heard everything!" Joe said as he shook his shoulders.

"I know it sounds strange, but that is what I think happened." said Ben, as he got up from the ground.

"Wipe off as much mud as you can, Ben, and let us continue. This storm cannot last much longer. No doubt it will run itself out very shortly." Zip announced loudly.

The men trudged on. Each man felt wet, cold, and at least one felt muddy. Each man had his own thoughts to help pass the time.

Zip thought about how beautiful Belle was. He hoped she would marry him upon his return.

Ben thought of a lovely warm bath and fresh, clean clothes.

Joe thought about the acorns his hands fingered in his pocket. He hoped the children in the cave would like them.

Chris thought about how proud his family would be of him when he returned home with their precious violin.

They continued on their way, with each man dreaming his own thoughts.

"There, it happened again!" exclaimed Ben, pointing at a rock.

"What happened again?" asked Chris.

"That rock moved out of my way! I saw it as plain as day." yelled Ben, as he backed away from the rock.

"Crackers, here we go again," said Joe, as his eyes followed Ben.

"Let us inspect the rocks and stones around here. Then, we can be sure of just what is happening." Zip said, as he approached the rock.

"I will stand here, and you check." Ben jestered.

Zip approached a rock. As he did so, the rock seemed to move away. The men looked at each other in awe and disbelief. Then, Zip continued after the rock. Again, it moved away.

"You were right, Ben, these rocks do move. They do not seem unfriendly, though neither do they seem friendly. I think we should try to walk around any stones or rocks we see," advised Zip.

"Let us go now." said Chris, nervously, "I will feel better when we leave this place."

Gingerly, the men tramped around the rocks, careful not to trip or step on them.

Suddenly, the men walked into a clearing. The sun suffused the shimmering air with warmth. Bluejay and his friends were sitting on tree branches singing merrily.

The men rubbed their eyes and looked around. They could not believe it.

"Where are we, Zip?" asked Chris, as he turned his head around. "Is this place on your map?"

Zip pulled his map out and spread it on the ground.

"No, Chris, this place is not shown on our map. The map ends here by those trees and does not continue into this clearing. We have something to add to our map." Zip announced.

Bluejay cawed and flew over to greet them.

"Hi there, Mr. Bluejay, it is good to see you again." Zip waved to greet him.

"What is this place, Mr. Bluejay?" asked Chris. "It is so beautiful."

The men looked around, first to their right side, then to their left side. They saw flowers of all colors, shapes and sizes. A marvelous fragrance filled the air. They spied a bushy-tailed squirrel and two rather large chipmunks sitting together on a log. Strewn here and there were rocks of various colors and sizes.

"Am I dreaming all this, Mr. Bluejay? Is this all real? We were in the middle of a fierce storm, and now it is so peaceful and calm. How can this be?" questioned Zip, as he scratched his head.

Bluejay cawed and put his head from side to side.

"Excuse me, sir," chirped a little voice.

"What? Who is speaking to me?" said Zip.

"I am, sir," said the little voice again, "Look down here."

Zip glanced down and saw a rock. It was talking to him.

"I really must be dreaming. Now a rock is talking to me. Chris, pinch me, and wake me up," whispered Zip.

"No, sir, you are not dreaming. We are Stonepeople. Because of the conditions in the forest, we have evolved into this form as a means of protection. The violent rain and wind do not bother us because we are covered with this hard outer shell," chirped the Stoneperson.

"Crackers! Then Ben was right when he said the rock moved," exclaimed Joe.

"We are glad to meet you and all the other Stonepeople," said Zip politely, as he glanced down to the ground. "But, we need a few minutes to rest and understand all of this."

"By all means, sir." answered the Stoneperson, "Do sit down and rest."

The men settled down on the green, thick carpet of grass.

"Those fellows over their are friends of ours. They will help you. Squirrel is a good runner and so are our friends, the chipmunk twins," said the Stoneperson, in his high squeaky voice.

"Glad to meet you," said Ben.

The animals chattered their response.

"We must get to Dom D. Dominic's house. He took our violin, and we must retrieve it. We have a large community waiting for us to return with our precious violin. Do you all think getting our violin is too big a job, or will you all be willing to help us?" asked Zip.

"We will help you," chirped, the Stoneperson. "Dominic is a selfish man. He does not live far from here. Rest, eat and stay the night, then tomorrow we will be off to Dominic's house."

"Very well. We feel grateful for all your help. Thanks, Mr. Stoneperson, Mr. Bluejay, everybody. I wish Zith and Tom could be here to help us," said Zip, as he rubbed his head.

The men ate. One by one, they dozed off to sleep in the glow of the firelight and the warmth of their newly found friends.

A RIDE ON SOME
NEWLY FOUND FRIENDS

CHAPTER 15

The squirrel chattered to the chipmunks as daylight arrived.

Zip sat up and looked around. For a minute, he forgot where he was. "Joe, Chris, Ben, wake up, we must be leaving soon," called Zip, through cupped hands.

The men yawned, as they slowly got up.

"I will make some breakfast for us," smiled Ben, as he took out his pots.

"Good morning, Stonepeople. How are you today?" asked Zip.

"We are fine, sir. Did you sleep well last night?" chirped a Stoneperson, in his now familiar voice.

"Oh, yes, thank you. It is very pleasant here," replied Zip, as he stretched his legs.

"Hi, squirrel and chipmunks. It is grand to see you again." smiled Zip, as he bent down to touch the warm, lovely fur of the squirrel.

The animals chattered their answers.

"All right men, gather around we must make plans. We have to figure out the best route to Dom D. Dominic's house. Our map has ended, so we are on our own." said Zip, pointing at the end of the yellow map.

"Do not worry, sir." admonished a little voice. "We will help you. The animals will carry you there. If you take a few of the smaller stones in your pocket, when you arrive at Dominic's house, you can place the stones on the ground, so they will ask other stones for help for you." Chirped the little Stoneperson.

"That is a good idea, little Stoneperson. We certainly will carry a few of your friends with us," smiled Zip.

Ben called the men to supper.

The Stoneperson walked, in a zig-zag manner, over to the animals. "Are you fellows ready for this trip?" he asked them.

The sound of gibber-jabber, confirmed the animal trio were ready.

"Where did Mr. Bluejay and his friends go?" Chris raised his eyes to search the trees.

"I do not know, sir," answered the Stoneperson, "But they will be back."

"How far from here is Dominic's house, Mr. Stoneperson?" inquired Zip.

"It is not too far when you ride on a fast runner's back," instructed the Stoneperson.

Pulling out his map, Zip spread it out in front of him, "I must draw this clearing onto our map. We must try to keep it accurate and up to date."

While Zip drew the clearing's details, the men filled their canteens with the clean, fresh water flowing in a babbling stream to the side of the clearing.

"Well, now the map is complete, up to this point," said Zip. "Is everyone ready to leave?"

"We are ready," chorused the men.

The animals jabbered loudly and hopped over to Zip.

"Which animal do you want to ride on, Joe?" asked Zip, with a smile on his face.

"Well, I guess I can ride on a chipmunk," but I'm not sure I like this, said Joe.

"May I ride with you?" asked Ben.

"Sure, if it is all right with the chipmunk," said Joe, shaking his head towards the chipmunk.

The chipmunk nodded his head and chattered his approval.

"I will ride on the other chipmunk," said Chris, this should be a fun experience.

"Fine, then I will ride on the squirrel. Let us climb aboard." Zip said, as he approached the squirrel.

"Do not forget a few small Stonepeople," reminded the Stoneperson.

"Oh yes, how could I forget these helpful fellows? I will pick them up right now," said Zip. "Any special ones to take?"

"By the way, do all the Stonepeople have names?" inquired, Zip.

"We do not have names now, because we are afraid of being identified by Dominic. If that were to happen, he would destroy our families, as well as us." Chirped the stoneperson.

"I am sorry to hear that, but we will try to help you someday, to escape this outrage." Promised, Zip.

"Two small Stonepeople, please come forward. We must help these men to get their violin back from Dominic," commanded the Stoneperson.

Two small Stonepeople zig-zagged forward.

"You both know what to do when you get to Dominic's house?" asked the Stoneperson.

"We do," tattled, the Stonepeople.

"Let's climb aboard now, men," decreed, Zip.

Zip climbed up onto the squirrel's back. It felt warm, soft and cozy.

Joe mounted the chipmunk and held on to his neck.

Chris is up next. Then Ben. But, as Ben goes up he knocks Joe off. Now Ben sits on the chipmunk's back, and Joe lays on the ground.

"Are you all right, Joe?" called Ben.

"Yes, I think so. Be more careful, please. I would like to get there in one piece." retorted Joe.

"I am sorry, Joe. It was an accident." Uttered, Ben.

Once again, Joe climbed upon the chipmunk.

"Are we ready now, men?" asked Zip.

"We are," chorused the men.

"Goodbye, Stonepeople. Thank you all for your help. Please thank Mr. Bluejay when he returns," said Zip.

Then, off they went, with every man holding on tightly.

ON TO DOMINIC'S HOUSE

CHAPTER 16

"I hope these animals really know the way to Dominic's house. If they do not then we are lost," thought Zip.

The animals and riders came out of the clearing into another part of the forest. Again the tall trees blocked out the view of the sky. The weather was clear, no rain in sight. On they went. The animals were very agile and easily jumped over the exposed tree roots.

Zip looked around making a mental note of his surroundings. He had to list them on his map.

The squirrel ran first, followed by the two chipmunks.

"Hang on Ben," yelled Joe, "Let us not have any more accidents today."

"I am holding on so tightly that my knuckles are turning white. I really do not plan on falling to the ground," replied Ben.

"How are you doing Chris?" called Joe.

"As well as can be expected," answered Chris.

"Zip, do you think it will be a long ride to Dominic's house?" asked Ben.

"I am not sure Ben, so just to hold on and hope it will be a short ride," shouted Zip.

A warm wind blew up and the tall trees began swaying their branches back and forth.

"Do you think we will have another storm Joe?" asked Ben.

"Let us not worry about it until it happens," answered Joe.

A few hours later the squirrel and chipmunks slowed down to a trot.

"Be alert men. We may be at Dominic's house soon and we do not know what we will find when we get there," warned Zip.

The animals slowly walked over to some high bushes and stopped. The men looked over the animals heads. There directly in front of them stood Dominic's house.

It was a large stone castle. Grey in color, with a white and purple flag waving in the wind, from a flagpole on top of a donjon, the large inner tower in a castle. Around this castle was a moat. When the front gate comes down it forms a bridge over this moat and makes an entryway into the castle.

The men climbed down from the animals' backs and walked around to the front of the bushes. No one said a word. The sight of the castle was overwhelming and all the men could do was to stare at it.

Squirrel hopped over to Zip and nudged him in the back.

"What, oh yes squirrel, we are all right. We just did not expect to see such a large structure. We live underground so this is all new to us," said Zip.

"Let us sit and rest a bit," said Joe and I will make some coffee for us."

The men sat facing the castle. Squirrel and the chipmunks lay down to rest under the shade of the bushes.

"Do not make any coffee Joe, just give us something cold to drink. It is better if we do not light a fire. The smoke may draw attention to us," said Zip.

"By crackers, you are right," said Joe, "I never thought of that."

"How will we get over the water to the castle Zip?" asked Ben.

"I am not sure. We must walk down to the water and look for a way," replied Zip.

Joe gave each man a glass of a cool, refreshing drink.

"My that was good," said Chris, "What was in it Joe?"

"That was mushroomade." replied Joe.

"Mushroomade?" chorused the men.

"By crackers, every time I try something new you always question it," said Joe.

"We question it, but we eat it, don't we?" asked Zip.

"Yes, I am glad to say that you do," answered Joe with a grin.

"Come men, let us walk down to the water. There must be a way to cross the moat. We just have to find it," said Zip.

The animals stayed behind, nibbling on some juicy grass, as the men walked down to the water.

"We must find a way to cross this moat or we will never retrieve our violin," said Zip.

As the men walked along the edge of the water, they saw some ducks. There on the water sat two female and two male mallards.

"Do you think that they will help us to cross this moat," asked Ben shyly.

"We can ask them," said Zip.

"Excuse me ducks, would you come over here? I would like to talk to you," called Zip.

The ducks swam cautiously over to the men and sat there looking at them.

"We are small and do not weigh very much. Will you carry us across this moat to the island of the castle? asked Zip.

The ducks looked at each other and then quacked. The men took this to mean yes and became confident again.

"If you can walk up onto the bank, good friends, we can climb onto your backs," said Zip.

The ducks stepped up onto the bank. Zip climbed up and then Chris. Next came Joe. Finally Ben was up too.

"Be careful men not to fall off into the water. Here we go. When we get to the island, take care and get off safely. Then take cover because we do not want to be seen yet," said Zip.

Off the ducks swam bringing the men closer to their goal.

BLUEJAY & FRIENDS ARRIVE

CHAPTER 17

"I am glad that this water is calm," said Chris, "I do not know how to swim."

"Neither do I," said Ben.

"Just hold on tightly and do not think of falling off," Zip said.

"A little further more and we will be on the opposite shore," said Joe.

"What happens when we get there?" asked Ben.

"We will look around and decide what to do then," said Zip.

As the ducks reached the shore they walked out of the water onto the grass.

The men climbed down from the ducks backs.

"Thank you ducks for the ride. It was so good of you to help us. If we can be of any help to you sometime just look us up," said Zip.

The ducks turned and swam away leaving Zip and his men on land.

"Hurry men and take cover. When we are sure that no one has seen us we must then fan out and look for a way into the castle," said Zip.

The men hid in the shrubs and waited. It seemed like an hour before Zip said, "All right men, I think we can start to walk around and look for a way into the castle. Be careful and remember Dominic can crush us like a brown leaf."

"I will go with Joe," said Ben.

"You are welcome to come with me, Ben, but please no more accidents," said Joe.

"Chris, you and I will stay together. Let us be off now. In one hour's time I think we should meet back here under these shrubs to report our progress. Agreed?" asked Zip.

"Sounds good to us," said Joe and Ben.

Joe and Ben walked to the right and Zip and Chris walked to the left of the shrubs.

"This castle is very big. It is made of many stones both large and small. I do not think that we can ever get inside of it," said Chris.

"We must try. We can not disappoint all our friends," said Zip.

Just then Zip saw something in the sky. It was approaching the castle.

"Hide Chris, there is something coming in this direction," called Zip.

The men dove for cover in the bushes and watched. As the shape in the sky came closer, the men could see that it was a formation of birds. It was Bluejay and his friends!

Zip was so happy to see the birds. He felt safe to know that Bluejay would be there to help them.

"Chris look, it is Bluejay and his friends. Let us run down to the shore and meet them. I hope Joe and Ben will see Bluejay and then come back to the shore," said Zip.

The formation drew closer. Then they dropped down and flew low over the moat. They came to rest near the shore.

Zip and Chris came running from the left just as Joe and Ben ran from the right.

When the four men came together they received another surprise. There climbing down from the birds' backs were Zith, Tom, Peter, Ted, Sal, John, Jimmy, Bert, George, Matt, Jerry, Scott, David and Ned.

Zip ran over to the new arrivals and hugged as many as he could reach. When he came to Zith he said, "I did not want to leave you Zith, but your foot was in a bad way. I am so happy to see you well again. I am so happy to see all of you."

"Mr. Bluejay you really are a good friend of ours. Once again you came to help us. Thanks," said Zip.

The birds and the men walked from the shore to the cover offered by the shrubs.

"How is it going men?" asked Peter.

"We just arrived here a little before you did. We are looking for a way to get inside the castle," replied Zip.

Bluejay cawed.

"I am sorry Mr. Bluejay, but at this time you can not help us. If Dominic sees you he will know that something is going on. We must do this alone. Perhaps you can help us later," said Zip.

Mr. Bluejay cawed.

"How is Belle?" asked Zip.

"She is well and waiting for you to return," answered Peter.

"I hope her answer will be yes when I return to her," Zip said, as his face turned pink.

"That remains to be seen," said Peter with a smile.

"Now that we are all here, we must decide upon the plan of action. It will not be an easy thing to get into this castle. It will be even harder to take our violin back. Do you have any plan of attack yet?" asked Peter.

"Well no, Peter, we will think of something though," replied Zip.

"We can not use the birds to fly over the castle walls because Dominic would see them and we would not have a chance to defend ourselves. I am sure that he would shoot us down. We can not lower the moat." said Zip.

The Wee Cave Men sat in a circle trying to think of a way to get inside Mr. Dominic's castle. The walls were too thick. The windows were too high. The door was on the other side of a deep moat and they were very small men!

"What are we to do?" they wondered.

SLIPPING THROUGH
THE CASTLE WALL

CHAPTER 18

While the Little Cave Men were resting and trying to decide how to get into the castle, Peter sat down beside Zip.

"How did you find this castle, Zip?" asked Peter. "I do not remember it being listed on our map. In fact, I do not remember the map listing anything past the forest."

"Our map did not show us the way. As we walked through the forest we walked into a terrible storm. We thought it was the end of our journey and also the end of us. Then we came to a clearing and it was beautiful. It was warm and sunny. Bluejay and his friends were there and after staying with us for awhile Bluejay left to get you and bring you here to us. While we were in this clearing we met a group of Stonepeople.

"A group of what?" interrupted Peter.

"Yes, a group of Stonepeople. Due to the conditions in the forest these Stonepeople developed hard outer coverings to protect themselves. They introduced us to a squirrel and twin chipmunks. It was the squirrel and the chipmunks who brought us here," said Zip.

"I see," said Peter.

"The Stonepeople! That's it! Why didn't I think of them before," yelled Zip.

"Are they here too?" asked Peter.

"Yes, a few of them are here in my pocket. See," said Zip, as he pulled them out of his pocket and held them in his hand.

"What can they do to help us? The castle is very big and they are not strong enough to break it down," asked Peter.

"We can show you a way into the castle," said a little voice.

"It spoke!" said Peter.

"Yes, they can speak. They are good friends of ours. Please help us little Stoneperson or we will never retrieve our violin," said Zip.

"Put us down over there near the castle and stand back," said the biggest Stoneperson.

Zip did what the Stoneperson directed and called to his men to step aside.

The little Stonepeople walked over to the castle's wall and looked around. Then they walked up to the wall and talked awhile. The Stonepeople moved back from the wall and walked over to Zip.

"We have arranged for you and your men to walk through the wall. Some of our Stonepeople are a part of the wall. Whenever you give us the signal we will call to the Stonepeople in the wall and they will step out of the wall and leave an opening for you and the men to enter the castle," said the Stoneperson.

"How did the Stonepeople get into the wall." asked Zip.

"Many years ago Dominic decided to build a castle. He could not find enough bricks around here so he decided upon rocks. We could not all run away fast enough so some of us were placed into the wall. That is why we will help you. We do not like Dominic any more than you do," said the Stoneperson.

"If they tried to escape he would kill their families. So they have never tried to leave the wall. Whenever you give us the signal we will call to the Stonepeople in the wall and they will press themselves close enough to leave a small opening for you and the men to enter the castle," said the Stoneperson.

"So that's how Dominic keeps the Stonepeople prisoners in the wall," said Zip.

"I am sorry for your friends that are in the wall, but I am glad that we met you," said Zip.

"Unbelievable," said Peter.

"Crackers," said Joe.

"When shall we go in?" asked Chris.

"Right after supper will be a good time. It will be a little darker then and we can slip around inside the castle unnoticed," said Zip.

Tom and Bert started making supper while the men sat around and talked.

"We must be careful once we get inside the castle. If Dominic sees us we are goners," warned Peter.

"Each man will take a partner and stay together at all times. There is strength in numbers so do not get separated from each other," said Zip.

"Has anyone here ever been in a castle?" asked Ben.

"No, none of us have," replied Joe.

"Do not be afraid of the castle. It is big and we are small, but if we stay together and be mindful of the danger, we will succeed," reassured Zip.

"Supper is ready," called Tom, "Come and get it!"

The men ate a good supper and then started to regain their confidence.

"We can do it," said Bert.

"I'm sure we can," Ned agreed.

"We will show Dom D. Dominic that he can not take something that is not his," said Scott.

"Let us clean up and start our quest," said Zip.

"We must stay in pairs. We number 18 in all. That makes 9 pairs of men. Square off men and be counted," said Peter.

The men paired off as partners:

Chris and Ben	Joe and Zith
Ted and Jerry	Jimmy and George
John and Sal	Bert and Matt
Scott and Ned	Tom and David

"That leaves us Peter," said Zip, "We will stay together."

"All right men, you all have a partner. Let us get started," called Zip.

"Give the signal Stoneperson, and we will start," said Peter.

The Stoneperson gave the signal and a few large stones rolled out of the wall and left an opening twice the size of the tallest man.

"Here we go men, be careful," warned Zip.

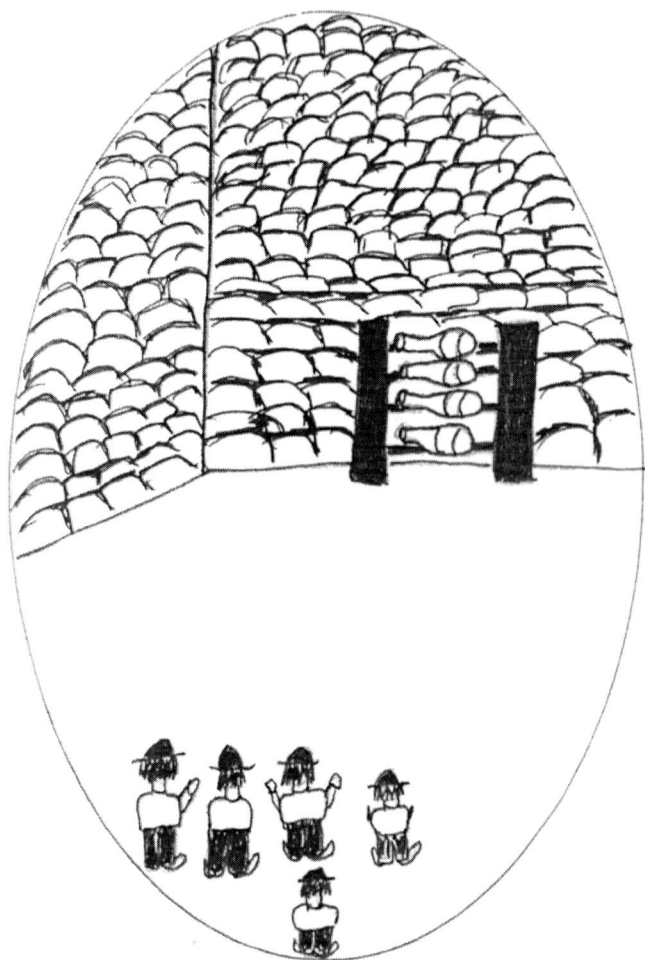

THE LOCATION OF THE VIOLIN

CHAPTER 19

"Move slowly and silently men, try not to be seen," said Zip.

The men slipped through the wall and stood quietly on the inside of Dominic's castle.

"Where are we now? What room are we in?" asked Tom.

"We seem to be in a wine cellar judging from the wine bottles in these wooden racks," answered Zip.

"This is a perfect place to have entered the castle. We will find the stairs leading up and see where they take us. Once we are upstairs we must look around the castle for the place to keep a violin collection. No one is to make a move without consulting the rest of us. We do not want to be hasty," said Zip.

"Here is the staircase," called Tom.

"Let us go," said Zip.

Slowly the men climbed the staircase. At the top of the stairs stood a heavy wooden door. The handle was too high for Zip to reach.

"Zith, is your foot all healed and feeling like its' old self?" asked Zip.

"It sure is," answered Zith, "Why do you want to know?"

"We will have to climb on each other's shoulders to reach the door handle and you being the widest will make a good foundation for us," laughed Zip.

"Oh, all right," agreed Zith.

Zith stood directly under the handle of the door. Zip climbed up on Zith's shoulders, but he still could not reach the handle. Then Tom climbed up on Zith and shook back and forth while trying to maintain his balance. Slowly he climbed up until his feet were on Zip's shoulders.

"Can you reach the handle?" asked Zip.

"Yes," said Tom nervously.

"Go ahead then and open the door. Do it quietly. We do not want to be seen yet," warned Zip.

Slowly the door creaked open. First a crack and then a few inches wider. Tom and Zip climbed down.

"There does not seem to be anyone around," said Peter.

"Let us move out of this cellar while we can," advised Zip.

The men walked single file through the big doorway. They did not make any noise because the floors were heavily carpeted.

"This is a beautiful place. I wonder how many people live here," said Joe.

"I hope not too many," answered Tom.

"I think that the violin collection would be kept in a living room in a showcase. Don't you?" asked Zip.

"Yes, that would seem like a good place for it," replied Peter.

The men walked down a long corridor, passed several closed doors and hoped the doors would not open.

"There is a staircase up ahead. Dominic may be up there so let us walk carefully," warned Zip.

The men started up the stairs. Suddenly they heard talking.

"Quick men, hide under the carpet there at the end under the railing and stay silent," whispered Zip.

The men slipped under the carpet just in time.

Dominic, dressed in a leather suit with high leather boots, and his wife were walking down the stairs talking loudly to each other.

"It looks great in your violin collection, Dear, and I know that you love it. So what is the trouble?" said Dominic.

"If only you did not take the violin, the trouble is that you stole it. All this time I thought you had bought it for me, but now I find that you stole it from a group of people who tried to be your friend. How could you? If only you did not take that violin. I am sure you have made many people unhappy. It is so beautiful and I love it, but I do not like keeping other people's things," said Mrs. Dominic.

"But Dear," started Dominic.

"Never mind. I do not want to listen to you," said Mrs. Dominic and she walked down the stairs, turned and slammed the door.

"Women! I will never understand them," said Dom as he walked down the hall and out of sight.

"Mrs. Dominic is not so bad," Zip said. "It sounds like she never knew that the violin was stolen,"

"The violin must be upstairs. Let us go and look," said Peter.

The men climbed out from under the carpet and hurried up the stairs.

At the top of the staircase was another hall. The floor again was carpeted and chairs lined the walls and pictures hung on the walls above the chairs.

"It is now time to split up. Go together in pairs and good luck men. Remember no move is to be made until we all meet and talk about it. In one half hour we are to meet here again. If we have located the violin we will then decide upon the best way to retrieve it. Good luck men," said Zip.

The men split up and went in different directions.

"We may as well look into the room directly in front of us Peter," said Zip.

The men walked slowly towards the door. Just then a person who looked to be a servant of Dominic's came out of the room. Peter and Zip ran under a chair for cover. The servant walked on.

"Whew, that was close," sighed Zip.

The men reached the doorway. Zip pushed and the door opened up to reveal the dining room. Fine china and crystal were set out on the table along with shiny silverware and candle sticks. This was all set on an elegant linen tablecloth.

"They must be having company tonight," said Zip.

"That will make our job harder because now there will be more people to hide from," said Peter.

The two men looked around the dining room, but did not find a showcase.

"It is time we returned to the stairs. Let us go," said Zip.

When Zip and Peter returned to the appointed spot, they found Chris and Ben, Joe and Zith, Tom and David, Ted and Jerry, Jimmy and George, John and Sal, Bert and Matt all waiting for them.

"Where is Scott and Ned?" asked Zip.

"They have not returned yet," answered Joe.

"Oh, here they come now," said Tom.

"Any luck men?" asked Zip.

"It is a beautiful castle, but we did not find any showcase," answered Joe.

"We could not open a door down at the other end of the corridor," said Ned, "That is why we were late."

"Then you did not get into the room?" asked Peter.

"No, it will take three men standing on each other's shoulders to open the door," answered Scott.

"That must be the room we are looking for," said Zip.

"I think it is locked," offered Ned, "It does not move at all."

"Now that we have found our violin's location, for surely it must be behind locked doors, let us go back down to the wine cellar. We will hide there until the party starts and then make our move," said Zip.

The men moved silently back down the stairs to the wine cellar.

THE PLAN OF ATTACK

CHAPTER 20

"Here's the wine cellar's door. Now we will see for sure if Dominic and his wife are in there. Stay out of sight until I signal for you. My signal will be a white handkerchief that I will wave through the doorway if the room is clear," said Zip.

"Be careful," advised Peter.

"I will." Zip said and off he went.

The door was ajar when Zip walked up to it. He listened and all was quiet so he gently pushed the door open, stepped through the doorway onto the stairs. He noticed a lantern shining from somewhere below. Cautiously, he descended the stairs. On the last step he stopped and listened. He could not hear any voices, but he could still see the lantern throwing shimmering shadows on the wall. It was eerie and Zip could feel his heart beating so fast he feared it would jump right out of his chest. Slowly he inched down from the last step and started walking towards the lantern. He looked over his right shoulder and then his left. No one was there. Zip heard a noise, but could not tell what was making it. Slowly he went on tiptoes into the room. The noise became louder as Zip came nearer to the lantern. Suddenly the source of the noise was directly in front of him. Zip stopped, then he laughed and sat down to rest on a box.

"It is only a pipe with a leak that is dripping onto the lantern and making all that noise and I thought that it was a ghost," said Zip to himself.

When he recovered his spirit and he was sure that he was alone in the cellar, Zip climbed the stairs and gave the "all clear" signal.

The men came into the wine cellar and closed the big door behind them.

Zip led the men down to where the lantern was sitting on the floor. The men sat Indian style around the lantern and relaxed.

"Soon we must make our move. I am sure that Mrs. Dominic will show off her violin collection when her company arrives. That means she will unlock the door. We must be ready to run in and hide in that room until she returns the violin and locks the door again," said Zip.

"It is a dangerous job men. If anyone wants to back out, now is the time to do it," said Peter.

"Raise your hand if you wish to leave and we will understand," said Zip.

Not one hand went up.

"Good, then we are still together in this mission?" asked Zip.

"We are," yelled the men.

"A few of us will go back through the wall and look for Mr. Bluejay and his friends. When they are found, you will return to the castle wall and wait for our signal. It will be my white handkerchief waving to you. Then Mr. Bluejay and his friends will fly up to the window and carry us away with our violin. Is that clear?" asked Zip.

"Yes, but which men are to leave?" asked John.

"You can pick five men and yourself—if that is all right," answered Zip.

"Very well. Ted, Matt, Jerry, Ned and Scott will come with me," said John.

"Agreed," said the men.

"When you find the birds, tell them how important it will be to be quiet. If we can take our violin back without a fight, I would like that. Mrs. Dominic is a good woman and I would not want to see her get hurt," said Zip.

"I have a few biscuits left if anyone would care to have a bite to eat," announced Tom.

"Would we!" said the men as they gathered around Tom to share the biscuits.

"We can help ourselves to a little liquid refreshment from the apple cider barrel over there on that low shelf. After what Dominic has put us through to retrieve our violin, he owes us a little refreshment," said Peter.

"After we have eaten we will get ready to return upstairs. Remember men there will be more people around to hide from. If they see us before the door is unlocked, we may never retrieve our violin," said Zip.

"The violin will be in a showcase. We will have to stand on each other's shoulders to reach the doorknob to open the showcase. Zith, I am afraid you will have to be on the bottom again," said Zip.

"I was afraid of that too!" said Zith with a smile.

The other men laughed.

"It is a good thing that Zith hurt his foot," said Peter, "Otherwise we would not all be here to help."

"That is right," said Zip, "Whenever you plan on hurting your foot again Zith, first make sure we need help and then go right ahead."

The others laughed and Peter patted Zith on the back.

"The night is wearing away. We must get ready to leave the safety of the wine cellar," said Zip. "John, you and the other five men must leave now. Find Mr. Bluejay and wait outside for our signal.

"Right," said John, "Let us go men."

The men pulled on their hats and buttoned their jackets.

"Goodbye and Godspeed," John said as he shook hands with Zip.

"Now it is up to us men. We must move as quietly as possible. We will succeed if we pull together and I am sure that we will," said Peter.

"Here we go and luck be with us," said Zip as the group ascended the stairs.

ALL HANDS PULLING TOGETHER

CHAPTER 21

"Once we go through this wine cellar door we can not turn back. We have agreed to continue, so we will, but please be careful," said Zip.

The men opened the great door, sneaked inside and listened. They could hear music being played somewhere upstairs. Many feet were dancing in time to the music. Voices could be heard, but what they said could not be distinguished.

"There are many people upstairs so be on your toes. Do not make any noise to draw attention to yourselves. Here we go then," said Zip.

The men walked swiftly down the corridor to the flight of stairs leading up to the party.

"Remember, if you must hide do it fast so you are not seen," warned Peter.

The men crept up the stairs. When they reached the next to the top step they could see bright lights shining from a large doorway halfway down the corridor.

"Duck quickly," whispered Zip.

The men stood against the riser as a servant passed by the stairs.

"Crackers, that was close," said Joe.

"He did not see us. So far we are safe," Ben said.

"Sh, isn't that a familiar tune?" asked Zip.

The men stood still and listened.

"That is our violin. It is still so beautiful. Belle will one day play it again and she plays it so beautifully," sighed Zip, a tear glistening in his eyes.

"We will continue on to the room that Ned and Scott told us about. It is in this direction. If Mrs. Dominic is using our violin the door must be open now. Let us go," said Peter.

Single file the men climbed up the last step and ran for cover under a chair. They drew back against the wall as another servant walked past.

"Whew," said Jimmy, wiping his brow.

The men walked along the corridor hugging the wall and staying under the cover of the chairs. They came to the large ballroom and carefully peeked in.

They saw two large chandeliers both brightly lit. Under these chandeliers danced beautiful women dressed in lovely full flowing gowns. They were dancing with men who were wearing handsome suits.

"Hurry past this doorway, go one man at a time. We must move while we can," urged Zip.

Ben looked around, saw no one and ran past the opened door. Once on the other side, he dove for cover under a chair. Each man in turn did the same thing until all the men were past the doorway except for Tom.

Tom stood pressed against the wall with his eyes wide open.

"Come on Tom," whispered Zip. "You can make it."

"I am coming," said Tom.

He carefully looked both ways and started to cross over. In the middle of his crossing the band stopped playing and everyone in the room started to applaud. Tom became frightened, he fell down on the floor amidst the many feet of the guests.

The men stood staring and were hardly able to breathe.

"Come on Tom, creep over here. You are almost here now," coaxed Zip.

Tom looked up, but did not move. He was frozen with fear.

"Hurry Tom. If they find you our mission will never be completed," whispered Peter.

"Roll over on your side and just keep rolling," urged Joe.

Tom rolled over and over until he was finally out of the doorway.

"Crackers! That was close," sighed Joe.

"Are you all right, Tom?" asked Zip.

"I...I...I think so. I am sorry, I just got scared," chattered Tom.

"It could happen to anyone," Peter said. "Now let us move on."

The men hurried down the corridor until they found the right room. Here the men stopped.

"It sounds quiet inside. I hope there are no people inside because here we go," said Zip.

Zip pushed the door and it cracked open. Tom swallowed hard. The men stood back.

"I will go in first. If it is safe I will call you," said Zip, and in he went.

Directly in front of a window stood a large showcase. The back of the case was made of wood and the sides and front were made of glass. Inside were many violins. No one was in the room so Zip called to the men. They came in and closed the door behind them.

"I feel a little safer now," said Tom.

"Good, but remember we are not home yet," said Peter.

"We must climb up to the window and open it up. From the window we can get our bearings and see if Mr. Bluejay is there yet," said Zip.

"I will be the foundation again. Come on men climb up and be careful not to fall," said Zith.

The men made a totem pole of themselves. First Zith, then George, then Ben, then David, then Sal, then Jimmy and finally Zip on the top.

"Hold still men while I open this window," said Zip.

He leaned over and opened a hook that held the shutters closed. A cool breeze came in as the shutters opened.

"Do you see any of Dominic's men out there?" whispered Peter.

"No, not yet. It is a little early anyway," said Zip, "But this window gives us a good view of the moat and the forest through which we came."

The men climbed down.

"We must hide and wait now. John will find Mr. Bluejay and he will help us," said Peter.

"I hope so," whispered Tom.

"Over here by this wall it is warm. We can rest here and wait," Jimmy said.

Eileen M. Foti

The men waited. It seemed like hours to them. Then suddenly, they heard footsteps in front of the door. The men ran over and stood behind the showcase as the door flew open.

RETRIEVING THE VIOLIN

CHAPTER 22

"You played your violin superbly tonight Dear," said Dominic.

"Thank you, but you mean the "Small Peoples" violin, don't you?" asked Mrs. Dominic.

"Come my Dear, after all this time you are certainly the owner of this little violin," said Dom.

"Just how do you figure that?" asked Mrs. Dominic.

"Well, if the "Small People" wanted their violin back they would have come for it a long time ago," answered Dom.

"You may have scared them or any number of other things may have prevented them from coming for their violin. If I ever see them again I will return their violin to them," said Mrs. Dominic.

"Not I. I would fight them for it. It is the only violin like it in the world and now it is ours," said Dominic.

"You are wrong, but I am too tired to stand here and argue with you. Goodnight, I am going to bed," said Mrs. Dominic.

"Goodnight," said Dominic.

Mrs. Dominic left and Dom turned to replace the violin into the showcase. Just then Tom felt a sneeze coming on. His nose started to twitch and his mouth started to open and he thought he would give their location away.   Zip turned and noticed what was happening to Tom. He quickly placed his hand over Tom's nose and stifled the sneeze.

Dominic, not aware of the men's presence in the room, placed the violin in the showcase and closed the door.

"Just let them try to get this violin.   I would fill them full of arrows," he said.   After saying this he turned, switched off the lights and left.   The men heard Dominic locking the door and footsteps walking away from the room.

"Crackers, that was close," sighed Joe.

"Do you think he will be back?" asked Tom.

"I hope not.   Let us get started now.   First we must climb up and look through the window again," said Zip.

Up went the men until Zip was looking through the window again.   He waved his handkerchief into the breeze and waited a few minutes.   Then he waved it again.   The men were starting to get nervous.   Zip thought, "Maybe John could not find the birds, maybe they did not want to help.   Maybe…"   Just then Zip heard something flap and he strained his eyes to see.

Mr. Bluejay flew onto the window sill.

"Good to see you Mr. Bluejay.   We were getting nervous, but I guess we really should not have," said Zip with a smile.

"Wait there Zip and we will pass up the violin," called Peter.

Peter watched as a few of the men climbed up and opened the showcase door.

"Be careful," warned Peter, "We must not drop the violin."

"Chris reached into the case and lifted out the violin. Then pass it to Tom and Tom pass it to Joe and Joe pass it to David and then David hand it to me," said Peter. "Then I will pass it up to Zip."

So it went. Down one stack of men and up the next.

The men climbed down from the showcase just as the violin reached Zip's hands.

"I have it. Finally it is safe in our hands again. Now we must leave this place and return to the cave with our valuable possession," said Zip.

"We must use you as we would a ladder," said Peter, to Zip and the men, "Or else we can not reach the window."

"Come Peter, climb up here. You will have the honor of carrying our violin home," said Zip.

Peter climbed up and soon was standing on the window sill.

"Mr. Bluejay call over one of your friends to carry Peter down to the forest floor. The birds and men can wait there for us. When we are all there we will leave as a group for our home," said Zip.

Bluejay cawed and a young blue jay flew onto the window sill.

"Climb aboard Peter and good luck," said Zip.

"Thank you. Come as soon as you can to join us," Peter said as he flew off on the bluejays back.

"Keep your friends coming Mr. Bluejay, we must not waste time," urged Zip.

Soon Joe, Tom, Chris and David were winging off to join Peter.

"Now Mr. Bluejay, there are seven of us left. This poses a problem. We are not tall enough to reach the window sill if we do not climb up on each others' shoulders. How will the last men on our column get out?" asked Zip.

Bluejay cawed and a small blue jay flew into the window and landed on the floor.

Zip stood on the window sill as the other men climbed down to the floor.

"Climb aboard Ben and hold on," called Zip.

The bird flew out of the window and passed another blue jay coming in. This continued until only Zith was left standing in the room and Zip was standing on the window sill.

"One more Mr. Bluejay and we too can leave," announced Zip.

Another bird flew into the window. Zith backed up to give him some room to land and instead he slammed backward into the showcase. The showcase fell over with a crash.

"Hurry Zith, get on the bird, we must leave fast," yelled Zip.

Just as Zith climbed onto the bird he heard the key turning in the lock of the door.

"Hurry, hurry," yelled Zip as the lights were switched on, revealing Dom D. Dominic, standing there with his bow and arrows. When he saw the broken showcase he became very angry. Dominic started to load his bow as Zith and the bird flew out through the open window.

Zing! The arrow flew after Zith, but did not hit him.

"I think we had better leave too, Mr. Bluejay. Goodbye Dom D. Dominic, thank you for our violin. Your wife will be glad to hear that we took back what rightfully belonged to us," called Zip.

Zip could hear Dominic yelling as he shot arrows through the window after them.

"Give me back that violin or I will crush you all!" shouted Dominic from the window.

"No you won't," said Mrs. Dominic, because if you do I will never speak to you again."

"This is a happy day for us Mr. Bluejay. We have waited so long for this moment.

We could not have done this without your help. Thanks for being our friend. We will always be grateful to you," shouted Zip.

Off they flew to join their friends in the forest and to start the happy journey home.

JOURNEYING HOME

CHAPTER 23

"Over here Zip," called Peter, "We are all safe and waiting for you."

"Wonderful! This is a great moment for us. We have done what we set out to do. Now we must return home and share our happiness with our loved ones," said Zip.

"Do you think Dominic will follow us?" asked Tom.

"No, I think Mrs. Dominic will not permit him to. She really did not like the idea that he stole our violin and if he wants to keep peace in his marriage he had better never bother us again," answered Zip.

The bluejay landed near Peter and Zip jumped down to greet Peter and the animals awaiting their return.

"Oh, hello Mr. Squirrel and hello Chipmunks. We really appreciate your help. It would have taken us a much longer time finding Dominic's castle without you," said Ben.

The animals chattered their approval.

"Let us hurry to the clearing inside the woods. I can cook a feast and we can properly thank the animals and the Stonepeople," said Tom.

"Crackers, that is a good idea," agreed Joe.

"So be it," said Peter. "On to the clearing Mr. Bluejay and join our feast."

"Do you remember where the clearing is Mr. Bluejay?" asked Zip.

Bluejay cawed.

"Then fly over the trees and bring us together with our wonderful friends," called Zip.

The squirrel and the chipmunks ran off toward the clearing. The men climbed aboard the birds again and the birds flew off.

In a little while the birds landed in the warm, sunny clearing.

"Hello Stonepeople, how are you? Did your people from the castle return home?" asked Zip.

"Yes, thank you. We are well and we are glad to see that you made it and are well too," answered the Stoneperson.

"If it was not for those Stonepeople near Dominic's castle, we never would have retrieved our violin. For this we are forever grateful," said Zip.

"It was our pleasure," answered the Stoneperson.

"Come Tom and start cooking our feast. We are starving after our stimulating escape," called Peter.

"Yes Sir," said Tom.

Tom cooked whatever he could find that was edible. He made soups and salads from mushrooms and greens and found delicious berries growing nearby for dessert.

"Come and eat. Let the feasting begin," yelled Tom.

Everyone ate and laughed together, man, animal and Stoneperson. It was a fantastic feast.

"Let us sing while we feast," yelled Chris. "We have not been so merry in quite awhile."

So the men sang:

"We did what we started out to do
Took back our violin that is true,
Now we are feasting and thanking each friend
For helping to make this mission so happily end."

Where is our violin now Peter? I would like to see it. Is it still shiny?" asked Zip.

"I have it in this small leather case. Here it is. One thing we can say about Mrs. Dominic is that she took good care of our violin.   Look how shiny it is," answered Peter.

"If Belle were here she could play us a tune. No one plays a violin as well as Belle does. Do you agree with me, Peter?" asked Zip.

"Yes I do, but remember I am her father so naturally I would think that she plays the violin well," said Peter.

"I will help clean up the dishes Tom," called Bert, "Two can work faster than one."

"Very well and thank you," Tom replied.

In a short time the work was finished and the men were ready to leave.

"Mr. Bluejay will you carry us home?" asked Zip.

Bluejay cawed.

"Pack up men and climb aboard our feathered friends' backs. They will take us home," Peter said.

"Goodbye Squirrel and Chipmunks and thanks again for the ride," said Ben.

"Crackers! You gave us a fine ride," smiled Joe.

The men said goodbye to the Stonepeople and climbed aboard the birds.

"Come Zip, what is keeping you?" asked Peter.

"I am just finishing our map. I must bring it up to date now that we know what is after the forest. Our ancestors did not venture that far, therefore, they did not complete this map," said Zip.

The last line was entered and Zip carefully refolded the map and placed it in his pocket.

"Ready Peter? Now we can leave," called Zip.

Good-byes rang through the air as the birds lifted off the ground. The men waved and then held on tightly to the birds' necks.

"Fly high over the trees Mr. Bluejay. Soon we will be home. We can once more enjoy life, we can once more enjoy our music and food. This is a good day," said Peter.

"When I hear Belle's answer it will be a better day," said Zip.

Then on they flew, each man with his own thoughts, each bird with his own happy rider.

ARRIVING HOME

CHAPTER 24

"It really is cold up here, Mr. Bluejay, but it sure beats walking," said Zip.

Bluejay led the formation of birds winging their way over the forest.

The men held on tightly, but this time they were even brave enough to look down.

"It is a beautiful view from a bird's back. You birds are lucky to be able to fly any time you wish too," sighed Tom.

"We are making good headway. It will not take very long to return back to the cave," Peter shouted to Zip.

"Yes, we will be there soon. Hang on, we would not want to lose you now," said Zip.

On they went until suddenly Bluejay began to caw.

Zip looked down and saw a familiar sight. There up ahead was the cave.

"We did it, we made it home," Zip yelled to Peter.

"So we did," replied Peter.

The birds landed on the hillside turning the green grass to a blue, white and black cover.

The men climbed down from the birds and stretched their legs.

"Thanks Mr. Bluejay. If we can ever help you please let us know. We owe you and your friends a great deal. Can you stay awhile or do you have to leave?" asked Zip.

Bluejay cawed, placed his beak upon Zip's shoulder and then slowly flew off. The other blue jays followed and the grass returned to green.

"Is that you Zip," yelled Sam. "I will call the others," and with that he hit a gong that had been placed near the cave entrance. "We placed this gong here as a special way of announcing you," said Sam.

People started arriving at the mouth of the cave. Smiles lit up their faces. Everyone hugged and kissed and shook hands and cried and laughed, all at the same time.

"Let us go into our home for we wish to show you all something," said Peter.

All the people returned to their homes, even Sam left his post for this special occasion.

"Everyone sit down please," said Peter, "I will show you something special. Many of you have never seen our violin before and many of us have. Well, now we can all see it," and as he said this, Peter pulled the violin out of the little leather case.

'Ah, Oh and Crackers," could be heard above the applause.

Pat walked over and kissed Peter on the cheek. Peter hugged her tenderly.

Belle started walking over to Peter and accidentally bumped into Zip.

"Oh, excuse me Zip. I did not see you standing here," said Belle.

"That's all right," laughed Zip.

They both laughed.

Belle continued walking to where Peter was standing.

"Play us a tune Dear," said Peter.

"I think Danny should sit next to me while I play, if it was not for him we would never have thought to retake our violin," Belle said.

Danny blushed and sat down near Belle.

"Come on Tom, bring your ocarina and Chris your drum. Casey bring your oboe and let us make some lovely music once again," called Belle.

Zip stood by the doorway and proudly listened to Belle magnificently play the violin.

When the selection was over, everyone applauded loudly. Then Zip walked over to Belle and took her hand. They walked into the hall, stopped and faced each other.

"Belle, you told me you would give me your answer upon my return with the violin. Have you made up your mind if you will accept my proposal and become my wife?" asked Zip.

"Yes, I have made up my mind," smiled Belle.

"What is the answer then?" asked Zip.

"The answer is yes. I will be proud to be your wife," answered Belle.

Zip's face broke out into a wide grin. "I will be a good husband and love you more and more each day," said Zip.

The happy couple embraced and then walked back to inform the others of their wedding plans.

When they arrived back with the others, they found Joe on the floor showing the children how to spin the acorn tops that he had picked up and saved for them.

When Zip announced the wedding plans, Tom started to play the Wedding March and everyone congratulated the happy couple.

So once again the little community of the wee cave people was happy; peace and love was found again, at the end of the cave.

ABOUT THE AUTHOR

Eileen M. Foti was born in Brooklyn, New York and was one of four children. She moved to Tappan, New York, in Rockland County, after she married Charles Foti. Eileen has three children and two grandkids.

Taking photos of nature has always been a favorite hobby and has won Eileen many ribbons in photo club contests. Eileen has also exhibited her paintings throughout the area.

She graduated from Dominican College with a degree in English. Writing has always been a pleasure for Eileen. She had two books published last year and is excited about this new book.

Eileen lives with Charlie and Kiltie the Scotty and Bonnie the Westie. They are great company. Of course, the grandkids, Cary and Mia, are the hands down favorites.